Yea! Wildcats!

ODYSSEY CLASSIC

Yea!
Wildcats!

JOHN R. TUNIS

An Odyssey Classic
Harcourt Brace Jovanovich, Publishers
San Diego   New York   London

Text copyright 1944 and renewed 1971 by Lucy R. Tunis
Introduction copyright © 1989 by Harcourt Brace Jovanovich, Inc.

Requests for permission to make copies of any part of the work should be mailed
to: Copyrights and Permissions Department, Harcourt Brace Jovanovich, Publishers,
Orlando, Florida 32887.

Library of Congress Cataloging-in-Publication Data

Tunis, John Roberts, 1889–1975
Yea! Wildcats!/John R. Tunis.
p. cm.
"An Odyssey classic."
Summary: A young, idealistic basketball coach taking over a high-school team at
mid-season tries to turn it into a first-rate team despite opposition to his methods
by business and political leaders.
ISBN 0-15-299718-0 (pbk.)
[1. Basketball—Fiction.] I. Title.
PZ7.T8236Ye 1989
[Fic]—dc19 88-30040

Printed in the United States of America

A B C D E

Introduction

John Tunis, who wrote umpteen books and hundreds of articles about games, did not care a whole lot for sports. He did care a great deal about the players, as well as about the people who watched them. Throughout his 50 years as a sports correspondent and sports novelist, Tunis learned a hard lesson: contests that focus solely on winning often bring out the worst in a person. *Yea! Wildcats!* is perhaps the best novel we have about the slick sins adults can commit—and excuse—in the name of "spirit" in games played by their children.

Of course—as anyone who has read his baseball novels knows—Tunis was devoted to the *good* qualities sports could bring out in people. His books are always full of folks doing the right thing and gaining just rewards. But for that he did not credit sports so much as he credited human nature. Sports are just a field in which the human drama is played out in its most elemental form, giving people a chance to show strength of will, intelligence, creativity, compassion, cleverness, humor, unselfishness, and—more than anything else—the dedication to teamwork that Tunis felt were necessary and natural for proper functioning in *all* activities. If Tunis so desired, he could have written books about a pottery studio or an automobile plant that showcased exactly the same human strengths. He saw them everywhere—and just happened to pick sports because he lived in the sports world.

Or *was* that all there was to it? *Could* pottery elicit anything like the shocking deceit practiced by adults with regard to a high school basketball team in *Yea! Wildcats!* Do assembly-line workers manipulate and scheme as frantically as the town fathers in Springfield, Indiana, where the Wildcats play? The answer, for Tunis, was probably "No." Because sports mean little in the larger scheme of world events, they provide an opportunity for simply decent behavior; they should be so *easy* to do right. But we keep letting them tempt us into the worst kind of twists of values, and instead of using their true nature as a safeguard against meanness, we turn them into major passions that demonstrate human folly.

Yea! Wildcats!, the story of a small Indiana city that goes stupid over its high school hoops team, was not originally supposed to be the gripping, high-minded tale it turned into. It was supposed to be a nice, classic good-guys-win story of schoolboy basketball in the heartland. Tunis had written a few such sports books already, to great effect, working his moral lessons rather subtly into the texture of very realistic entertainments.

Because accuracy of atmosphere was very important to this well-trained sports reporter, Tunis spent part of a season in Indiana. Wanting to get just the right setting, the right cast of characters, the right skein of feelings, he went to a small Hoosier city to soak up background. He attended basketball games and followed the fortunes of one group of cagers all the way through to the state tournament. And what he discovered turned his nice-story-to-be into a different book entirely, a serious, significant novel that should have remained before us for 40 years as a warning and an indictment. To call it prophetic is not enough. Our surprise has still not caught up with the shocking reality Tunis coolly presents here. Consider this: The scandals that keep rocking the juncture between sports and education today are all about *colleges*, where most athletes are adults; in *Yea! Wildcats!*, Tunis revealed the same unscrupulousness at the heart of high school athletics. We're still not ready to examine this frightening reality.

The book is brilliant, reverberating throughout with the angry shock Tunis must have felt when he saw the dark side of the rah-rah. In Don Henderson, Tunis created the perfect character to reflect his own innocence and disillusionment: a talented young coach whose genius lies in the conviction that the way to win is to let the boys play the way they naturally will if the pure simplicity of the game is opened up to them. Implicit is the belief that they will likewise perform best—in sports and in life—if they remain in touch with the pure simplicity of their own nature. Henderson is very wise about kids, perhaps because he isn't far from being one himself. Certainly, among the shifty Springfield adults whose "maturity" centers on their belief that they can control other people, he seems to be of a different generation, if not species. He gets the chance to prove his distinctiveness—and that of the kids on his team—in a wonderful series on confrontations that supply as many sports thrills as a reader could wish, but with the keener edge of serious adventure.

Has Tunis turned into a moralist? Is the let-sports-be-sports simplicity of his earlier books lost for good? Yes—and no. Certainly *Yea! Wildcats!* is a book with a moral. But because the sins on which he focuses arise from a sports milieu, he is in effect still saying,

"Let sports be sports" and, more important, "Let kids be kids." Along the way he touches on many of his pet peeves—racism, conservatism, the tendency of the middle class to knuckle under to its wealthiest members, the adverse power of group conformity. He also creates the finest representative of one of his favorite character types, the Flinty Old Sage. Peedad Wilson is a treat in this role. One has the feeling at the end of the book that we haven't seen the last of him, that Tunis won't be able to resist bringing him back. And we are right: *A City for Lincoln* is just around the corner. But for now this book is enough. Indeed, in light of the sports scandals we keep uncovering every year, it may even prove too much.

—Bruce Brooks

Yea! Wildcats!

1

The three members of the Springfield School Board leaning over the front row of the balcony were the only collected persons in the building. Most of the time they were less interested in the shifting, changing pattern below than in a young man at the far end of the gymnasium. He was seated on a wooden bench and flanked on each side by two youngsters in playing clothes.

A shrill cry rose. It turned into a shriek, overpowered everything and everyone, took possession of the arena, burst into a roar as one small Center Township player, dribbling cleverly, swung down the floor, pivoted, faked, and then cutting in beneath the basket hooked it up. The ball fell through cleanly. As though in protest at this insult to the home team, the electric scoreboard blinked furiously several times.

CENTER TWSHIP 31   SPRINGFIELD 31

The roar became a Niagara of noise. The sound drowned out the yells and cheers from the stands, the cries of individuals shouting from all sides, the stomp-stomp of feet on boards, the hoarse, quick cries of the players. The attention of the three men was drawn momentarily to the game itself.

"Lookit him . . . lookit that Jerry Kates go! Isn't he something! Dribbles so slow they just can't stop him," said the man on one end of the trio. "Last year he was a farm boy shooting baskets against the barn door. Now lookit him! Why doesn't Kennedy develop kids like that here at Springfield?"

J. Frank Shaw on the other end leaned over.

"I understand he only weighs a hundred and six pounds. After that game against Greentown he was down to a hundred. And his dad . . . say, his dad is something. Dave was keeping score in the Greentown game, and seems when it was over his dad comes up and asks for the kid's average. 9 out of 13! Think of that; 9 out of 13! The old man, he just shook his head and says, 'Well, he warn't used to that-there gym!'"

The floor below was in a frenzy now, both sides on their feet yelling for a goal.

"Watch that Center Township coach," said the big man on one end of the trio. "Takes it cool-like."

"Yeah," Shaw answered. "He's cool all right. 'Bout the only cool person round here. If only he wasn't so young . . ."

The man in the middle of the trio had not spoken. Suddenly he pointed to the floor. Time was called and a midget of four or five rushed out, pushing the towel box on wheels. He had blond hair and wore a yellow sweater half concealed under blue overalls, and he was about as big as the object he pushed before him. Across the floor he went, toward the circle of sweaty players panting in the center. They leaned over the box, lifted the lid. On the inside were painted the words:

SPRINGFIELD WILDCATS

Following the tiny figure below, the man in the center of the three spoke for the first time. "Cute, ain't he?" The others did not share in his approval.

"He's cute all right, Peedad. Trouble is, you can't figure to use him in the line-up. I only wish his dad was as good a coach as . . ."

"Now, you take what Don Henderson's done over to Center Township," interrupted Peedad Wilson. "How many boys do you suppose he's got, Tom?"

"Not more'n seventy, seventy-five, mebbe. See there, he only has four subs with him tonight."

"Seventy boys in the entire school. Suffering cats!" Peedad shook his head. "And lookit that slippery little forward there, developed from nothing."

"Don's a good coach, nobody denies that. If only he wasn't so darned young." The two men on each end exchanged comments when the whistle blew and the teams drew together for a jump ball.

A fever of emotion ran through the hall. "C'mon, Jack . . . get in there!" "Take it away from him. Get that ball." "Cover . . . cover . . . cover up." "The old fight, Center, move the ball . . . move the ball!" "Cover, Wildcats!" And from the floor below a steady, shrill cry:

"FIGHT-TEAM-FIGHT, FIGHT-TEAM-FIGHT, FIGHT-TEAM . . ."

The three men glanced with interest at Don Henderson, the Center Township coach on the bench. The quiet figure sat erect between his four substitutes who were leaning over, their elbows on their knees. Against his mouth he held a rolled scorecard. His lips were tight. His face was young, yet old, for he carried the strain of the conflict in the frown of his forehead, in the tightness of his posture. But while the teams raced up and down the floor and the seconds ticked away and the excited mob called feverishly for a score, he was the calmest person in the gym.

"How much time?" asked the big man in the balcony.

"Minute. Less'n a minute. He could win, y'know, Frank."

"Sure could. He deserves to, anyway. Too bad he's so young . . . otherwise I'd be for him."

Then suddenly that quick shriek as the tiniest player on the Center Township team stole the ball and again dribbled it skillfully down the floor. He wove a kind of figure eight in and out among the bigger men who stabbed and plunged at him in vain. With a burst of speed he dodged a restraining arm, worked into the corner where he pivoted, passed out to the center, cut in and took the ball back, whirled, and with the same motion made a one-hand shot over his head.

For a second that was an age the ball hung on the rim of the basket. It fell through. The gun sounded. The game was over.

A mob of boys and girls swarmed out immediately upon the floor. They rushed their team, hauling them up and toward the basket. Now someone passed along a knife, and the first basket was slashed. Eager hands reached for the pieces. Then the other. The costumed yell leaders danced in, around, and through the crowd now spreading over the entire floor. The stands poured across the playing surface. The balcony emptied. Only those three men remained sitting as they had throughout the game, their elbows on the rail in front.

"Well, I'll be darned," said J. Frank Shaw, the good-looking man on the end. "I'll be darned. Springfield beaten by a Township High School with only seventy boys to pick a team from! Isn't that something? Now what'll we do? This can't go on. I think the young fella's good, myself. I'd be for him . . . if only . . . if only he wasn't . . ."

"If only he wasn't so young!" The man on the other end finished the sentence. "That's my feeling."

"Yeah. What do you think, Peedad? You haven't said a thing. What's your stand? The Board's gotta act; we can't permit this sort of thing to continue. How you feel about him?"

The little man in the middle, who had scarcely spoken all evening, stood up. Slender, of medium height, he was the kind of person you ordinarily would never notice. For a minute he watched the excited mob underneath, dancing, shoving, pushing each other in ecstatic delight; boys and girls, older people, businessmen, farmers in overshoes, all mixed up in that crazy quilt of emotion which swept the surface of the floor.

"I'm for him. He sure knows how to coach basketball. The kids like him and everyone over to Center Township speaks well of him. You two worryin' about his age, hey?"

"Point is he's really too young to coach at a place the size of Springfield. Kennedy was thirty-two when he came here, so was Pop Davis, and Jerry . . . how old was Jerry when he started? 'Bout thirty-six . . . or seven. Don's young for Springfield High."

J. Frank Shaw rose. "That's my objection. Too young. Right now he's too young."

"Well . . ." Peedad Wilson smiled. "Let's us go down and have a talk with him, anyhow. He may be young; but he'll get over that fast enough if he's basketball coach in this-here town."

2

No one would call the room luxurious. Actually the Springfield gym was hardly more impressive than the one to which Don had been accustomed at Center Township. For despite its size, not for years had Springfield enjoyed a winning basketball team; hence large field houses and elaborate gyms were something for the future. The room had lockers extending to the ceiling on three sides, sufficient for the team, the freshman team, the subs. There were two long wooden benches and a blackboard at one end of the room. On the blackboard half the court was outlined in white paint. The diagram showed the free throw line, the circle, the free throw lane, and the basket. At the moment it was covered with white chalk marks that looked like the tracks of birds in the snow.

Don Henderson stood beside the board, a piece of chalk in his hand. In his sweatshirt, open at the neck, and a pair of old trousers, he was almost as young-looking as the players. They sat on two benches which formed a V, the open end toward the coach and the blackboard, chewing gum, listening, watching, while he tossed the chalk in one hand and fiddled with the whistle, suspended by a string from his neck, with the other. The overflow stood behind the benches, watching and listening also.

"See what I mean? See there, Tim? You didn't watch that ball. No, you didn't, either. *Watch it*. Watch it onto your hands . . . watch that ball and you can't get hurt. Now, on that play there, that play which put Newcastle ahead in the third quarter, you were dead asleep, Denny, dead asleep."

The tall boy standing up behind one bench

with the sweater tossed over his back murmured something. The coach turned toward him.

"No excuses. I want no excuses, Denny. You were tired; you'd played two games that day; O.K., so had Newcastle. So had Wolters; but he pulled that sleeper on you, didn't he? Let's get this straight. We all make mistakes, bound to, but we'll have no excuses for dumb playing." His words hurt. The squad was not accustomed to this talk. Along the bench they stirred uneasily as he continued.

"There's some people here in Springfield were mighty discouraged about the team recently because we've done so poorly. I'm not discouraged. I know it takes time to practice plays; you gotta go over 'em and over 'em. You're a veteran squad and you know each other, but you've still a lot to learn. Most likely we'll have some more setbacks, but if you try I believe we can go places.

"Now this afternoon, start easy; throw 'bout eight or ten; you haven't thrown for a couple of days and you're kinda rusty. Then we'll begin working on those outa bounds plays for a while. And watch that ball; watch the ball, Tim. On that pivot there, Terry, let him come in fast . . . here . . . see what I mean?" The chalk did a staccato across the board. "See?" Then he stopped, and turning away from the blackboard faced them, speaking slowly and distinctly, looking hard in their faces.

"At . . . no time . . . take . . . your . . . eyes . . . off . . . the ball . . . at . . . no time. . . ." The room was still. They listened as they had never listened to a coach before. This guy wasn't like Kennedy. This Don Henderson was tough, really tough.

In Indiana the kids play alley basketball all year round. There are hoops over every garage door, hoops on the barns out in the country, hoops in halls and bedrooms in town. Boys start young. As soon as a youngster can walk, his father gives him the inflated bladder of a basketball and shows him how to toss it through his elder brother's outstretched arms. No coach in the Middle Land has to worry about material. His problem is to sort out that material, to get the best players and the right combination on the floor. That was Don Henderson's problem.

He looked them over. This was going to hurt, but it had to come. "Tom, this afternoon you go in at center. Denny, you'll take over Tom's spot on the B team. All right, le's go."

There was a burst of noise, the sound of

benches scraping on the cement floor, and the thud-thud of feet on the wooden stairs leading to the playing floor. Their voices concealed their amazement. But it was in every heart and on every mind. Tom Shaw for Denny Rogers! That kid Shaw for a veteran like Denny! A junior on the varsity instead of a man with two year's experience! Of course, his old man's on the School Board. He lives on the West Side of town. Of course, that's the reason; that's what this Henderson is doing. He's just nailing down his job!

But deep down they were worried. Denny Rogers out; who's next? Gee . . . am I safe? Is Jack safe? Is anyone really safe on this team? He's tough, this coach is, he's plenty tough; we never realized . . . why, he means what he says!

Three hours later, more tired and exhausted after the long practice than any of the players, Don finished his shower and dressed slowly. Russ Brainerd, the coach who helped with the subs, had gone, so he walked along to the Claymore where he usually ate dinner. The food at the Claymore was good. Because it was good, half of Springfield dropped in there once a week. Already, although he had only been the Springfield coach for a month, Don was a familiar face around town, known to everyone. He saw the time coming when in self-protection he would be forced to change his eating place for a more inconspicuous spot. The basketball coach in Springfield was fair prey for everyone in town.

He entered, spoke casually to several people at different tables, sat down, took up the menu, ordered dinner, and went to work on the *Evening Press*, hoping to be let alone. But Springfield considered the basketball coach public property. If you saw him, you stopped him and discussed the chances. There was also an off-chance that he might have an extra ticket for the Regionals or even the Semifinals toward the end of the season. Besides, if you were a male and therefore a former basketball player yourself, you could always throw in a helpful suggestion or two. That evening a man passed by, hung up his hat and coat, came past Don's table, and hesitated. Don looked up from his paper. The man's approach was cordial, his face mildly familiar.

Now, thought Don, I know this feller. Is he the president of Rotary or the man who helped me get a room or the banker who told me he used to play at Indiana U. or . . . Well, anyhow, he's a citizen of Springfield.

"Hullo, Don, how are you? Say, I was kinda

surprised you didn't play John Little toward the end over there at Newcastle. Them boys was getting pretty tired; coupla fresh men might have made a heap of difference."

"Yeah, John's a good boy. Has possibilities. But he's not quite ready enough in my opinion."

"Sure looks good to me."

Don fell back upon the question that never failed to deflate the drugstore coaches. "Mind if I ask how many games you've seen this season?"

It didn't deflate this stranger. "Well, none, to be truthful. But I've heard 'em all over the radio. That Buck Hannon is something on the air. And the game John got into last month, when he came in as a sub there, sounded to me he did all right. The kid's a scrapper, a scrapper from way back."

Don was tired. He was hungry. He was annoyed by the other's stupidity. "So he is. But we're in a basketball game not a prize fight, mister. Yes . . . that's mine, the roast beef . . . thanks."

The stranger turned back to his table. There, thought Don, I've probably made an enemy. Well, what's the difference? Besides, in this game you can't help making enemies. I found that out long ago at Center Township.

3

The coach's room in the gym was opposite and across the hall from the players' dressing quarters. Neither was luxurious. The room of the coach was small, about twelve by fifteen, lined on two sides with shelves that reached up to the ceiling. The shelves contained piles of towels, boxes of basketballs, of equipment, shoes, socks, supporters, shirts, and pants. Under the high window was a wooden bench running across the room which served as a rubbing table. Over the rubbing table was a sign:

Don Henderson had brought it with him from Center Township.

Beside the door of the room, which was opposite the window and the rubbing table, a small opening had been made through the wall into the hall outside. Red Crosby, the student manager, stood there, opening a carton of oranges. On the wide sill which projected into the hall was a towel, and on the towel a dozen red vitamin pills. After practice each player gobbled a pill and was handed an orange. Red wore a white sports shirt, open at the neck, and a blue sweater with a large red "S" upon it. His hair was auburn, he was distinctly on the fat side, and whenever anyone spoke to him he blushed and showed dimples on each cheek.

Don sat on the only chair in the room, pulling on his socks, when a man entered. On his arm was his overcoat. He wore a double-breasted suit, and seemed to know what he was about as he came in, one hand extended.

"I'm Fred Rogers, Mr. Henderson. Denny Rogers' father."

Red Crosby evaporated into the hall. Here's

trouble, thought Don, as he rose. When businessmen visit coaches, it sure means trouble.

"C'm in, Mr. Rogers, c'm in." He shut the door. "Sit down, sit down, won't you?"

The elder man leaned against the bench. "No, thanks. I was going past and thought I'd drop in and see about Denny. He's all broken up over this thing. You know, I'd kinda hoped the situation here would clear up when you took charge last month."

"So did I, Mr. Rogers. It will—in time."

"Yes, of course. You can't do these things in a hurry. But I wanted you to make my boy a player, a real player. What seems to be the trouble?"

"I'd like to see him come through, Mr. Rogers."

The elder man was unsatisfied. "Yes, but what's up? Last year and the first part of this season he was a regular. Now you throw him off for Shaw's kid when the season's only half over. I tell you, the boys are mighty upset. I've heard 'em talking up to the house."

"You want to know why your boy isn't on the varsity any more, Mr. Rogers?"

"Why, yes. . . ."

"I'll tell you why not. For one thing, he was

out dancing until two in the morning last Saturday."

"Oh, no . . . I don't think so."

"Mr. Rogers, I don't think anything about it. My business is to know these things, and I know what I'm talking about."

"Well . . . perhaps; but surely, one dance . . ."

"Nope, probably not; one dance doesn't really matter. But I ask my boys not to go to dances during the season and I expect them to obey me. If they don't want to follow the few simple rules I lay down, they don't want to play basketball very bad; that's all. And this isn't the first time Denny has broken training in the few weeks since I took over."

"H'm. I see. I merely wondered . . ."

" 'Nother thing, and p'raps I shouldn't say this to you, only since you asked you might as well know. Mr. Rogers, Denny has more native coordination than any player on the squad. He's a wonder with a ball."

"Well, then . . . why . . . what . . ."

"He isn't a team player. He won't play for the team."

"You mean he wants to be a star?"

"That's it exactly."

"But I should think you could train him . . . teach him . . . explain how . . ."

"I've tried, every way I know how. It isn't any use. He can't get along with the boys; he's got to be the whole thing or nothing. It's a tragic waste, because he could be what he wants to be and what you want him to be, if only he'd forget himself and become one of the team."

"Oh! I see. I didn't realize this."

"Mr. Rogers, things are bad right now. I know it perfectly well. It's always tough when a new coach comes in in the middle of the season. Some of the boys besides Denny haven't been training; we've lost several games we shoulda won, and I've had to take steps. I may have to do something more."

"I didn't know this. Maybe it'll teach Denny a lesson."

"I'd like to see the boy come through. He could be a fine player if he wanted to enough. It's right up to him."

There was a timid knock at the door. The elder man walked across. "Thanks for telling me, and thanks for being so frank. I wanted Denny to be a player real bad his last year; but I guess he's got to learn things the hard way, same as the rest of us."

"I guess he has, Mr. Rogers. Glad to have seen you. Hullo, Jack, come in."

The boy had a white sheet of paper in his hand. There was a strange look on his face as he said, "Hi, coach. This-here's for you. The boys wanted me to give it to you." He stuck out the paper and fled.

Russ Brainerd, coming in to dress, found him standing with the paper in his fist. Don said nothing but shoved it at him.

MR. HENDERSON:

We are upset about the team, and especially about the loss of one of the veterans, and our best player. We understand you are looking for future players; but on the other hand, what about a senior who does not have another year of sports to look forward to? We understand also that in bringing up an underclassman, you hoped to make us extend ourselves. But instead, one of the best men is neglected.

We have therefore decided not to practice until some step has been taken to remedy this situation. It is hoped you will see our side, and understand the grievances we have pointed out.

JIM SCHULTE

TERRY DICKERSON

JACK HOLMES

TIM BAKER

Russ glanced up, the paper in his hand, while across the hall the squad that had presented an ultimatum to its coach was waiting to play. Or not to play. The two men stood there, the new coach of an unsuccessful basketball team and his assistant, neither saying a word. No words were necessary, for both saw the problem they faced.

"Well! Only one thing to do!"

Brainerd's jovial features were sober now. "You'll stick your neck out. They sure love to win in this-man's town."

"We aren't winning now."

"You'll make yourself a-plenty of enemies. All these kids, their families and their friends . . ."

"That's part of being a coach."

"They'll say you've branded these boys for life."

He interrupted. "Russ! You want me to take him back?"

The other looked up. "I don't see quite how you can," he said slowly.

Don held out his hand. "Thanks. I needed that one. Well, here goes!"

The second he crossed the hall he felt the tense atmosphere of the dressing room. Usually it was noisy with the sounds and horseplay of boys dressing for practice. Now it was thick with silence. Four players in their street clothes stood around waiting the decision of the coach, while the subs, the juniors and sophs, pulled on their clothes, wondering.

Everyone glanced up as he stood in the door and, entering, closed it sharply. The paper fluttered in his hand, and his nervousness was visible to every player in the small room. It isn't easy to throw a veteran team out the window, especially for a young coach. And a newcomer, also.

"Fellows, I have your letter here . . . and I guess maybe there's been a misunderstanding. Seems like some of you boys don't realize what basketball is."

They were surprised. They were surprised and

a little complacent, too. Not understand basketball? Sure we do. Four fouls and you're out. A player shall not "hold, trip, charge, push, block, or use unnecessary roughness." Each quarter lasts eight minutes. After a free throw the ball is thrown from out of bounds by the opponent of the free thrower, provided the throw is successful. Not understand basketball? Why, sure we do.

"No, boys, I'm afraid you don't understand what basketball really is. Basketball is winning sometimes and losing sometimes. But most of all basketball is giving, giving all you got, giving every minute. That's one of the lessons of sport; you've always got something in reserve; you can always give more than you think you can. That's what you boys don't apparently realize."

They were confused. An uncertain look came to every face. Is he . . . is he going to be tough? Why, did we make a mistake? Denny said . . . we only meant . . . we didn't mean . . .

"Yes, you, Schulte, and you, Holmes, and you too, Dickerson, and you, Baker, all of you. Remember when we started this thing together, I explained we wouldn't have many rules, only a few simple ones; that I didn't believe in rules. But the ones we had you'd keep. Remember?

Now Denny Rogers forgot that; he's out. I caught him, caught him cold; caught him breaking my rules twice. Some of you chaps, though I haven't caught you, have been breaking rules also. Baker!" The word came suddenly. The blond boy snapped up.

"Were you at the Kappa dance until after midnight last Friday?"

"Nosir . . . that is . . . why . . . yes that is, just a few minutes, for just a little while."

"Schulte! Were you at the late movies the night before the Bedford game?"

"Why, no . . . I mean . . . I don't remember." A pause of a moment. "I guess so."

"I guess so, too." His voice was firm, like the set of his mouth. Now they were thoroughly frightened. They shifted uneasily on the long, hard bench. This wasn't at all the way they'd planned things.

"Dickerson! Someone saw you smoking in a poolroom on West Superior last Wednesday evening."

"Well, coach, y'see it's this way, it's like this. Now, I wasn't exactly smoking myself . . . I . . ."

He didn't wait. "Schulte! Dickerson! Holmes! Baker! Turn in your clothes."

No one spoke. No one moved. A colored boy

among the substitutes straightened up, and the bench on which he sat creaked.

"Jackson Piper!" The colored boy stiffened. "You'll take over one forward; Jim, the other. Mac, I want you in at guard; Chuck at the other one."

A sudden yell lifted the room. The unexpected had happened; the subs were going in. The sophs and juniors, who usually spent a year on the bench learning, were now the varsity. No wonder they yelled. Their cry was spontaneous and hearty. It stopped as suddenly as it began. For the four boys in street clothes were silent.

Why, he's tough, this Don, he's plenty tough . . . we never realized . . . he means what he says.

"Tom! You'll continue at center as you did yesterday. I wantcha to go out there this afternoon and hit Mac on the eye with that ball. Get me?"

The tall blue-eyed boy with the crew haircut nodded. There was an exultant look on his face.

"Yeah, coach. Just one question, please."

"O.K., what is it?"

"Which eye do you mean?"

4

It was in Don's second season as the Springfield coach that he really got to know J. Frank Shaw.

"Don, I'm going to call you Don, and I want you to call me Frank."

Somehow it didn't add up. Here he was, sitting in the Shaws' drawing room after a fine dinner, with the great man himself asking to be called Frank, Tom sitting in a chair with his long legs over the side, and Mrs. Shaw, knitting, on a davenport. These were good people, his people. He liked them.

As he sat there he tried hard to remember the things folks always said in Springfield about the Shaw brothers. The stories, the rumors, the reports he had heard ever since he was a boy, the stuff that everyone in Howard County repeated. They couldn't be true; they just couldn't. Here was the man that half Springfield called names, talking agreeably in his own home to an unsuccessful high school coach as if he'd known him all his life. These Shaw brothers were certainly not the ogres they were supposed to be around town.

"Tell me, howsa team panning out this year? You've got a better spirit, haven't you?"

"You bet! The boys are really trying. That's all I ask. Hey there, Tom?" The big boy grinned as the elder man, lighting a cigar, went on:

"You've lost a few games; well, don't let that upset you, boy. I realize what an uphill job you've had here. Situation was sure bad when you took over last winter."

"I didn't realize it at the time. I do now. You know, Mr. Shaw, when I fired those five boys last winter, I thought sure I'd lost my job. But the Principal was wonderful; he called me in and backed me to the limit; so did the Superintendent."

"They should," said J. Frank with emphasis. "Took nerve to do what you did."

"Maybe it wasn't courage, maybe it was desperation. Anyhow, I got letters and wires from coaches and principals all over the state. It helped make up for that dismal season we had."

"Wasn't your fault. Not a bit. I know perfectly well what you've been up against. Y'know, I used to play at Butler myself, time of George Stevens and Harry Thorpe and Ricky Farnsworth . . . why, we used to play to over a hundred thousand a year, even back in those days!"

"Frank!"

"Now . . . now . . . Mary Marcia won't let me talk about the good old days." He laughed and tapped his cigar on an ashtray. Don looked round the room, at the fire, at Tom dangling his legs over the side of his chair, at the oil painting over the mantelpiece of old Zadoc Shaw, or "Zadoc P." as he had been known round town. It was a painting of a long, not especially pleasant face. The man wore a high, stiff, old-fashioned collar; his eyes were light blue and unfriendly.

Don easily understood how Zadoc Shaw had come to Springfield from Western Pennsylvania in the '80s and died the richest man in town. And how some of the dislike attached to the hard-fisted pioneer had inevitably descended to his children.

Yet Frank Shaw was not like his late father. He was warm-hearted, open, friendly, and made a real effort to be a kind host. He was, too. On basketball, one of his pet subjects, he was also amusing.

"Nope, I'm not talking about my basketball days any more; she won't permit it. Anyhow, I'm expecting Tom will put me in the shade soon. But sometime when there's no one about, Don, you come up and I'll show you my den."

Don wondered how the stories about him and his weaknesses had ever started, why envious and jealous people spread such slanders without provocation. Surely a man of his kind . . .

The telephone outside sounded. J. Frank Shaw excused himself, rose, and went to answer it. "That's what it is, all day long," he murmured.

Mrs. Shaw flipped the knitting in her lap with annoyance. "He's on every board, every committee, everything constructive in this town. When anything has to be done, Frank is the one to do it. His brother Jack refuses to kill himself the way Frank does."

Tom shifted his legs in the big chair.

"We just see him at meals and basketball games," he said.

Don smiled as the elder man returned, sat down, and re-lighted his cigar. It was easy to warm up to him, as others who had met J. Frank had done before him. You could see the man knew basketball, and especially basketball in Springfield. Unlike most citizens of the town, he didn't expect the impossible.

"Now, Don, tell me how things are shaping up. I know you took over a mighty bad situation here, morale gone, and all that. I met Jack Holmes' father the other day; he was still griping about what happened last winter, and I just told him some facts. 'Ray,' I said, 'I saw your son down-town nights after eleven last year and, frankly, I wondered how long it would take Henderson to catch up with him.' 'Course he was furious, but he knew I was right; he couldn't say a thing. It was a bad situation, a real bad spot for you to be in. But you showed courage, for my book, and you acted just right."

"Yessir, it *has* been bad. It was tough last

season after I took over. This year I've got better spirit from these boys. I tell 'em, same as I told 'em out at the Township, it's up to them. I don't promise anyone a championship team; but I do say that if they want to make sacrifices, they can have a good team. I want good teams; I'm used to 'em, I usually have 'em."

The elder man nodded with approval. "That's why we picked you, Don."

"Yessir. Now, we had some bad luck over at Newcastle on New Year's Day. We lost that game by only three points after beating Logansport. That was our first good win, our first real win this season. In fact, since I came to Springfield. We shouldn't have lost that Newcastle game, should we, Tom?"

The boy shifted in his chair. The crew haircut waggled. "No, sir," he said.

"No, we shouldn't. Then trouble came. I lost two of my best boys with colds, and they were out when we played Anderson ten days later. They swamped us. I expected it. But I'm not the least mite discouraged, not the least. You can't go ahead faster'n you can in this game. I'm working 'em hard, and they're taking it. Fine spirit, Mr. Shaw, fine spirit these boys have, all of 'em."

J. Frank tapped the end of his cigar on the brass fender of the fireplace. "Frank," he said, raising his eyebrows and smiling. Mrs. Shaw smiled and Tom smiled. The visitor had to smile, too.

"Yessir, yes, Frank. Lemme tell you something. This team of mine is going to be a smart team before the season is over. They really think for themselves, these boys."

Again J. Frank turned the cigar round and looked at the end. "I'm glad. You're doing first rate; I've every confidence in you, Don. But now it's all settled, I must say I was sorta surprised last winter when you let Denny Rogers go and put that colored boy on."

There was a sudden constricted silence. Don felt uncomfortable for the first time since the maid had taken his hat and coat earlier in the evening. But he spoke firmly. "Jackson Piper was the best man for the place. But I'm glad you brought up that matter of Denny. You know, Denny storied to me several times; he wasn't keeping training, he was breaking rules."

"Oh! I see."

"More than that, Denny is spoilt. He's a wonderful natural player, one of the best in town. But he was hopeless on a team. I put Tom here, in. Tom took hold and has improved. He's not a natural player like Denny; maybe he'll be a better one on that account. Then right after came the revolt, you remember?" The elder man nodded.

"The spot was open, there was a place for Jackson Piper, so naturally he went in. I'll say he's made good, too!"

The big boy with one leg draped over the arm of the easy chair suddenly spoke. "I'll say! Where would we be now without Jackson?"

"Oh, I see, I see now. You know how 'tis; all sorts of stories get round town. I'm mighty glad to get the facts, although I've always had confidence in you, Don, and everything Tom here tells me makes me feel we're mighty lucky in Springfield to have got you."

"I'm glad to be here. Now. I wasn't very happy last year."

"I'll bet. Shoot, that telephone again." He rose and went out to answer the call.

"It's been fine meeting Mr. Shaw like this, Mrs. Shaw. I knew all the School Board over at Center Township; but this place is bigger, and I hardly thought the Board would take much interest."

"Oh, Frank takes an interest in everything.

He loves people, and he just wears himself out for this town. No one appreciates it," she sighed.

"Well, he's a grand person, and he really understands what basketball is all about. He doesn't ask for a championship team; he doesn't demand the impossible the way some folks in town do."

"Well, he knows the game. And he loves to talk about it. Next time you come let him take you up to his den and show you his trophies."

"Yes, I'd like to see 'em. When two old players get together, it's something. They say a man talks basketball in this State for an hour after he's dead. You know, I hardly met him that night last winter when he and Mr. Sherrill and Mr. Wilson came to our dressing room."

"Oh! That dreadful Wilson man. Isn't he awful? Have you been reading the things he's said recently in that nasty sheet of his?"

Don laughed with some slight embarrassment. "I rather gathered he didn't like your husband or his brother."

"He doesn't. You know he served a sentence in jail, this man Wilson."

Don was shocked. "In jail? Honest?" The thin, mouse-like figure of Peedad Wilson came to his mind. The third member of the School Board was hard to picture as a criminal. "Really? In prison? Well, how's it that he's on the School Board then?"

"Oh, I don't know. If you understood politics in this town, you'd see lots of things happen you didn't like, either. He's a Democrat, and according to law the Board has to be bipartisan and I guess he got on somehow. He just loves to fight. He fights Frank every chance he gets. And Frank's so patient, works with him on the Board and all the civic organizations just as if he never wrote those horrid things."

"Whatever Dad wants, Peedad wants something else," ejaculated the boy in the big chair.

"Exactly. Like your appointment."

"You mean Peedad Wilson didn't want me?"

"Of course. It was Frank who knew basketball and knew you could coach, so he fought and won. He never did convince the others until the night of that game last year . . . when was it?"

"The game when Center beat us over a year ago," said Tom, helping out his mother.

"That's right, over a year ago, it was. You see if Peedad was only fair, if he only told the truth, if he only told folks what Frank and his brother had done for the town. People here in town don't realize. They know about the memorial park, and the municipal swimming pool, and they know we gave the new Y and the hospital. But they never realize all the other things, the times we're called on, the summer camp for boys up river, and those things. Whenever there's a deficit for the community fund or the Red Cross, it's always Frank and his brother who make it up. Always." She flipped the knitting in her hands with an angry gesture.

"Is that so?" Here was a side of the Shaw brothers about which Don had never heard. These were the things folks didn't know or discuss, as she said. At that moment the big man re-entered the room.

"Excuse me, Don. Now then, tell me about the team, tell me some more."

"Well, there isn't much to say. Because they're young and inexperienced, and I never am quite sure what they'll do in a game. But they're grand kids with a grand spirit, the best ever."

"Are they? Why?"

"For one thing, they're coming; they're kids who were juniors and sophs last year. Then they'll really work. Take this boy, John Little. Last winter he was hopeless; but he tried hard and I spent some time on him. He improved, too, fast. Come spring, the boy asked me for special exercises and things he could practice on all summer. His dad built a hoop outside the garage; he took the exercises and practiced, and right now he's crowding two of my regulars."

"Is that right? I know John's father; fine chap."

"Well, that kid has it. He's a straight A student, too. But all these boys are different. They may not be better athletes than the farm boys I had over at Center, but they think better. They want a reason for everything, and I give it to 'em. I show 'em what I'm trying to do, and they go out and do it. Never have to ask 'em twice. Watch this boy Walt MacDonald; he'll be a star this year. Wait and see. He isn't scoring the points; but he counts out there, doesn't he, Tom?"

"You bet he does."

"They're a wonderful bunch, a wonderful bunch and I enjoy working with them."

Mrs. Shaw spoke up. "You make me understand why a man wants to coach basketball despite the headaches."

"There're plenty of headaches. But there's the other side, too. I guess only a teacher can understand, yet somehow there's a thrill to watching youngsters develop, watching them use what they've been taught and become poised and skillful. You know something? I get more of a kick when these kids, who've been battered around so long, win a game, than I used to on the team at college when we won."

"Do you? That's interesting," said J. Frank. "Maybe that's why you're a good coach."

"I don't know if I am. I doubt if those kids I fired last year think so."

"Enemies . . . you gotta make enemies."

"Don't I know it! A basketball coach has nothing else but, if he's any good. Better he is, the more folks he offends. I've been through all that. You get so you accept it as part of the game. Fact is, I believe the coach who doesn't make enemies doesn't make anything else, including the Finals at Indianapolis."

The cigar was poised in J. Frank's hand. Tom sat up straight in the chair. Here was this young fellow talking about the Finals at Indianapolis with a team that so far had hardly won a game all season. Meant what he said, evidently. His face was set, his mouth tight the way it was when he had faced the strikers on the team the winter before.

J. Frank looked at him closely. That's the kind

we need in this town, he was thinking. Trouble is the good ones all leave. They go off to Chicago and New York, and desert Springfield where they were brought up and got their education. I'm glad we got this boy, Henderson; he's the tough kind, the sort of a lad we need badly here.

5

Things were upside down. Everything was turned around. That night long ago, when the Board came down to the dressing room and asked him to coach at Springfield, he had been sitting on the bench of the visiting team. Sitting there and envying the home team its wealth of subs, subs, subs. Worrying for fear little Jerry Kates, his hundred-pound forward, wouldn't last out the game. Hoping and yet hardly daring to hope for a victory—and that greatest of all upsets, the triumph of a small Township school over a city team. Now things were upside down.

The gymnasium was neither enormous nor especially modern. It seated only 2,500, with bleachers on both sides of the floor and a balcony containing only five rows of seats. Yet he could remember how the place had overpowered him, how it had dazzled the Center Township boys the first time they saw it. Now the Hanson Gym was his gym, his home gym, familiar ground. Again Center was the visiting team, but it was no longer his team.

There's one thing to be thankful for, he thought. Jerry Kates has moved down to Evansville. Jerry was half that team. I won't have to worry about Jerry tonight. But they still have four of my boys left, and those kids are plenty dangerous. They know their basketball. They can do it—if we don't play like we know how.

A sudden outburst from the Springfield cheering sections swept the room. "Yea . . . Wildcats . . . yea, Wildcats . . . yea . . . Wildcats . . ." The noise drowned out the smaller Center sections opposite. The stands continued to shout as the Springfield squad trotted onto the floor. They wore satin shorts and sweaters of blue with the emblem of a wildcat on the upper left breast. It made them smart and elegant compared to the Center team in faded and much-laundered old uniforms. Moreover, they were taller and heavier, with twice as many players actually on the floor. They covered one whole end of the gym, spinning balls around, tossing them nonchalantly back and forth or shooting baskets with ease. The dozen youngsters of the visiting team were slender and small compared to their rivals.

"Wildcats . . . Wildcats . . . Wildcats . . . fight-fight-fight!"

Hang it, thought Don uneasily, as he watched his boys, I ought to work out a top-class team from this bunch if I'm any good at all. Look what I did with only a handful at the Township! In a way that makes it tougher, having this mob to pick from.

Two cheerleaders, each in white pants and a white sweater with a large red S on it, dragged a cage containing a stuffed wildcat to the center of the floor. The home crowd rose, shrieking with delight. They yelled, cheered, clapped hands, and stomped their feet in unison. The sound echoed and re-echoed from the roof of the ancient gym.

"Springfield Wildcats, clap-clap-clap . . . Springfield Wildcats, clap-clap-clap . . . Springfield Wildcats . . ."

We ought to win. This is the tough one. That game last night was a pushover; it didn't test the boys at all. I'd rather they hadn't played. It's this one, now, because whoever wins this afternoon will swamp Russiaville tonight. Darn it, we *should* win the Sectionals. I'm really counting on the boys doing that, at least. No one else in town thinks we can, but I've got faith in these kids. I believe they have what it takes.

The whistle blew, the referee waved his arms, and the team came toward the bench. The five boys of the varsity leaned over with him on the edge of the floor, sweaty hands interlocked. Though Don had not been exercising, his hands were damp, also. "O.K., boys, go out and play like I know you can. I wantcha to take nothing for granted this afternoon. I wantcha to play like this was the last game of the State Tourney. If you do, you'll win. I've confidence in you. Now go!"

"Le's go . . . le's go . . . le's go!" The stands rose as they raced out on the floor.

"Yea, Wildcats! Fight-fight-fight!"

The game started cautiously, each side feeling the other out. For the first quarter it was tight. From the bench, Don watched with apprehension as one team went into the lead and then the other. Outweighed and outmanned, the youngsters from Center hung on gamely. They worked into a lead, and at one time were six points ahead. Slowly Springfield edged up. In the front row of the balcony, Buck Hannon, owner and announcer for the Springfield radio station, turned the mike over to the man at his elbow for a commercial as the timekeeper's gun sounded for the end of the quarter.

He leaned toward Dick Lewis, the sports editor of the *Tribune*, at his other side. "Looks to me like mebbe our boys are going to find themselves this afternoon."

Dick nodded. "This Jackson Piper is a surprise to me. That colored boy is going great guns tonight. What's he made? Ten points already? And Shaw is something on those rebounds, isn't he?"

"Yeah. How tall is he, anyhow? Six-five? Well, a guy that big ought to be able to score a lot of points just by accident."

"But he's fast, too. Y'know, last year I thought

Don made a mistake when he chucked a veteran like Denny Rogers off the team. I thought this Tom was on there because he was his father's son, because he . . ."

"Because he lived on the West Side and his old man was on the School Board. So did I and lots of folks about town. We learned different, didn't we?" Like the president of the bank, the chief of police, and just about every male citizen in town, Buck knew as much basketball as any coach. Consequently, his admission that Tom Shaw had earned his place on the team was a concession. Buck felt himself a qualified observer.

So he was, too. Because as the game went on, the Springfield team edged slowly away from their rivals. With the half drawing to a close, Jackson Piper was running circles around the tired country boys, and it was evident that Springfield was the superior team. A lead of 24–17 at the half was satisfactory. The teams tramped down into the basement while the cheerleaders went to work on the rival crowds in the stands.

Back on West Mulberry Street, half an hour later, Homer Wilson let himself into his home, looked around, called out, and found he was alone. He went upstairs, put on an old coat and slippers, and came down to the sitting room where he picked up the bundle of newpapers he had brought in and sat down in an easy chair beside the radio. He flipped open the first paper, turned a page or two, and then suddenly looked up at the clock and snapped on the radio. Buck Hannon's delighted tones greeted his ears.

". . . Hatch of Center crosses the line with a bounce pass . . . it's Center outa bounds . . . Center outa bounds . . . to Hatch . . . to Davis . . . to Hatch . . . he shoots a long one . . . and misses. Shaw, the lanky pivot man of Springfield, reaches up under the basket . . . he grabs the ball . . . he has it off the bankboard . . . to MacDonald who comes down the court . . . over to Piper who dribbles past the ten-second line . . . past Hatch . . . he makes a burst of speed . . . say . . . is that boy fast . . . he passes over to Mac . . . who hands it to Tom . . . who slips it . . . there's Piper . . . he's got it . . . he's in there . . . he goes right in . . . and *makes it!*"

The roar drowned his voice. ". . . And . . . let's see now . . . the scoreboard is wrong . . .

that's Springfield, 42 . . . Center Township, 34. Folks, this team is really going to town . . . and that Piper lad is hot. There . . . a foul on Shaw, by Davis of Center . . . two shots, and are those Wildcats playing ball!"

Peedad Wilson filled his pipe. Looks like we didn't do such a bad picking job last year as some folks round town thought, no matter what they been saying about Don all winter. Well, that's how it is. If he wins tonight, he'll find he has a lot of friends in Springfield he never knew he had.

6

D on sat on the bench, his hands gripping his knees. Holy mackerel, we can't lose now! Surely we can't lose to a small crossroads school like Russiaville.

Trouble was they could. In his heart he knew they could, that in all sport nothing was so uncertain as the game you ought to win. He knew that his boys hadn't yet found themselves; that they still needed practice and more practice and more practice, drilling in plays, time to know each other better, to understand each other's peculiarities on the court. In short, time to become a team.

Yep, we could lose, even now. But we shouldn't. And if we win, golly, I b'lieve I'd rather win this one tonight than any game I ever played in at State. Or even that Springfield game when I was coaching Center last winter.

Out came the yell leaders before the bleachers. The gym was packed now, people standing at both ends and up back in the rear of the balcony, a larger crowd than in the afternoon when many businessmen were unable to get away from work. Not a seat, not a space vacant anywhere. Mr. Hinton, the High School Principal, wandered around, trying to find a place to squeeze in. Then the yell leaders, two girls in white sweaters and skirts, assisted by a small boy, did acrobatics before the throng. They saluted their rivals across the steaming gym.

"Hullo . . . Roosiaville . . . hullo . . . Roosiaville . . . we say . . . hullo!"

And Russiaville, with its small knot of supporters on the benches opposite, responded. The crowd rose yelling as the teams rushed onto the floor, the Springfield side in ecstacy over their team's triumph that afternoon. They foresaw a victory in the Sectionals, the first Springfield victory in several years. This was something like. Maybe that young fellow was a coach after all.

"Yea! Wildcats! Yea! Wildcats! Fight-team-fight!"

The game began. For a few minutes the Russiaville five upset them badly. They used delaying tactics and their tactics succeeded. Instead of allowing Jackson Piper a chance to break loose and shatter their defense with his speed and accuracy, they hugged the ball in the middle of the floor, passing it back and forth to each other, stalling, slowing up the tempo of the contest, attempting to upset the superior team. It worked. It often does. Springfield was dazed and uncertain. Watching from the bench, Don could hardly keep still.

Get in there . . . hang it . . . get in there . . . break that up, Walt . . . move that ball . . . Tom, why don't you take charge? There! There he goes! About time. . . .

Jackson Piper had the ball and was off. The room was hot from the afternoon's crowd and had not been well ventilated. So already sweat glistened and shone upon his skin. Gracefully he pivoted, faked a shot, passed the ball and then, taking it back, swung down the floor. He skirted the corner, went in, turned, whirled, and with an easy one-hand shot lofted the ball through the basket. Russiaville took the ball out, but Tom Shaw grabbed it and went down to score immediately after. At last they were off.

Yes, they were off, they were clicking, they were moving at last. Another basket and another. Once ahead, they went fast. Yet Don was still nervous. He heard Red Crosby, the student manager, at the far end of the bench, bantering with the Russiaville subs on the visitor's bench a few feet away.

"Red, if you don't stop needlin' those boys, I'll jam a basketball down your throat." Red collapsed into silence. The moment Don had spoken, he was ashamed of himself. Why, he was more nervous than the kids!

In a momentary lull around the arena, Buck Hannon's voice came down to him from the balcony directly overhead.

". . . At the end of the first quarter . . . Wildcats, 12; Cossacks, 4. For those of you who just tuned in, the Springfield Wildcats . . . *lead* the Roosiaville Cossacks at the end of the quarter,

12 to 4. Now it's the Kats outa bounds, with Piper bringing it in. . . ."

The score mounted. It mounted fast. So fast that even Don began to breathe. They were in it. They were in the Regionals; they were one of sixty-four teams to come through, only sixty-four out of the eight hundred who had started the Sectionals the previous day. Yet he even forgot this as he watched them in action. It was wonderful to see them stopped, upset, and then work out their own salvation right before his eyes. To see them think it through, grab the ball, and charge down the floor, deftly passing it from one to the other until Jackson Piper was in position to shoot. Then it was flipped to him and invariably dropped through the hoop. This was a team—at last. His hopes were justified. It was a team of fine, resourceful athletes. Without a star, too, unless you called Piper a star.

The timekeeper's gun sounded. The half was over. On the scoreboard were the figures: Springfield 20, Russiaville 8. The two squads charged for the dressing room and Don followed them, higher in spirit than he had been for many a month.

What followed was a slaughter. As the second

half progressed, Don began to pull out his best men. "Steve, go in there at guard for Mac. Wilbert, take over from Jackson Piper. Bill, you're in at center for Tom. Good work, Jackson boy, good work, boy; now go get yourself a shower. You too, Tom, that's fine work off those backboards there."

All the while the score mounted, for by this time the Russiaville team was worn down, beaten, weary, and exhausted. The score was in the eighties when the final whistle blew and the boys stomped noisily into the dressing room below.

"Wow! Whoopee! Wow! Boy . . . were you hot tonight! Hey, Jackson, you were sure handling that ball there!" They paddled into the showers, and the sound of splashing water was added to the ring of their voices.

"Hoo-ray for Tom . . . hoo-ray for Tom . . . someone in the bleachers shouted . . . hoo-ray for Tom!" They were all singing it together.

"Come, boys, get your clothes off . . . get those wet clothes off, everybody."

"Hoo-ray for Jack . . . hoo-ray for Jack . . . hoo-ray for Jack . . . he's a darn nice guy!"

7

Get in there! Hang it, get in there, Tom. Get that ball. Move, move . . . Jackson . . . shoot, back to Tom . . . now, Jackson . . . shoot!

Don was in there playing with the team, fighting furiously against the Bearcats, with someone tugging at his arm whenever he ran. As he ran he had to drag this person along at the same time, and when he wanted to shoot, it was necessary to shake him off.

Watch him, Walt . . . watch him, boy . . . don't

let him get in there . . . cover . . . cover . . . watch him alla time . . . now, there . . . Jackson . . . go on, boy.

They were off down the court together, passing the ball back and forth. But always that thing kept holding to his arm, pulling him back so he couldn't keep up.

The telephone! It was the telephone ringing that kept him back.

Don sat up in bed. The telephone's ringing. Great Scott, I've been asleep.

It was black. Downstairs the phone continued to jangle. Someone wanted him badly, and probably it was one of the boys in an auto accident or some sort of trouble. He climbed out of bed and went out into the cold hall. Sleepily he fumbled his way downstairs, grappling for the telephone on the table by the door. He hit and almost knocked it off the table. At last he got hold of the receiver.

"Yeah?"

"This Coach Henderson?"

"Uhuh."

"Coach, this Pete Smith. I wasn't able to reach you last night. Reason I'm a-calling you this time o' day is, I wanted to be sure and get hold of you. Now you don't know me; I work on the early shift at the General Motors plant, and I'm on my way to work right now. Coach, I usta play on the team myself back in '35, and I sure would like to get my hands on . . . to follow those boys over to Marion this week if . . ."

Don cut off the flow of words. He was too tired and too sleepy to be angry, but he stopped the man.

"Sorry, but I don't aim to get tickets for anyone. It's a hard and fast rule of mine."

The man paid no attention. "Coach, I'm a citizen of this-here town, and I'm a-counting on you for those tickets, that's all."

Don yawned loudly into the telephone. "Look! I tell you I have a rule. I don't get seats for anyone."

"Yeah, well, I'd only want two. One for me and one for my brother-in-law in Tipton. I told him I'd get him one, so you'll hafta do something."

Don put down the receiver. There's another one of the enemies they talk about. Can't help it. Cold and annoyed, he stumbled through the darkness and up to bed. With some difficulty he discovered by his watch that it was 5:15. No wonder it's still dark. With a groan he sank under the covers.

However, by this time he was wide awake. He heard the clock downstairs strike six, but he must have been asleep later for the jangling of the telephone woke him up again. Once more he stumbled through the blackness down the steps. His watch said 6:45 as he picked up the receiver.

"Don? How are you, boy? This is Bill Higgins over to Center Township."

He was torn between disgust at being yanked again from his bed and an ancient friendship. The ancient friendship won.

" 'Lo, Bill."

"Don, I'm just mighty sorry to get you up so early. Y'see, we're all going over to Richmond to spend the day with my wife's family, and I wanted to talk to you before we leave. Think you could hook me a coupla tickets for Saturday?"

Again he yawned into the telephone. "Why, Bill, I'd sure like to, but you know how things are. Same as over to Center. I don't get tickets for anybody, not even my old friends."

Old friends, it appeared, were more reasonable than strangers. "Why, sure, I know how 'tis. I see. Well, mebbe you'll hear of a pair round town. If you do, remember me, please."

"Uhuh. I will. *If* I do. But I'm not promising anything."

"I know, I understand. Well, thanks, Don, thanks. And good luck to you over at Marion this week." The conversation ended. Don put down the receiver, turned to go upstairs, took a couple of steps, came back, lifted the receiver from the hook and placed it on the table beside the telephone.

Now mebbe I'll be able to get me a little sleep.

•

The next afternoon Don sat in the only chair in the coach's room, putting on his socks. Red Crosby was counting towels, and Russ Brainerd stood bouncing a ball on the concrete floor. There were only three of them and a single chair. The more chairs, the more people in the tiny space; the more people, the more confusion. Hence one chair.

"You going over Friday night?" Russ kept his attention on the bouncing ball.

"Take 'em over Saturday," replied Don, turning the other sock inside out and slipping it over his toes. "Rather have 'em sleep in their beds Friday night."

"Early?" The two men knew each other by this time and seldom wasted words.

" 'Bout eleven-thirty. We'll take five cars: yours, mine, the Shaws', old Smith's, and maybe one behind as reserve."

"O.K. I'm having mine overhauled. Be ready Friday noon."

"Good! Why . . . hullo there, Tim. How are you?"

A boy stood in the doorway, grinning. He wore a sports coat, a shirt open at the neck, and a pair of gray trousers. Tim Baker was the only junior of the five boys who had been suspended the year before and the best of the lot. Now what, thought Don.

"Can I see you a sec, Don?"

"Why, sure, come on in." Russ slipped through the door, followed immediately by Red Crosby. Don shut the door and started fastening his belt as the boy stood before him.

"Don . . I just wanted to say I'm sorry about what happened last year. I'd like to get back on the team if I could."

"Tim, I'd sure like to have you. But if I take

you back now, it means throwing someone else off. How would that sit with these kids, d'you think?"

"I know, Don, but it was all Denny Rogers who started the trouble last year, you know that."

"Wait a minute, Tim. You had two chances. You were warned like everyone else."

"Yes, but, Don . . ."

"I don't have many rules; I dislike rules. But those who don't obey 'em, get out. Win or lose."

"It doesn't seem to me fair to penalize us all for the ringleader."

"Look here! Were you at the Kappa dance that week when the trouble blew up last year?"

"Yes, I guess so."

"I warned you, didn't I?" The boy said nothing. "Funny thing is, had you asked me for late permission, I'd have given it to you. You didn't; you sneaked off and went to that dance and thought I wouldn't catch you. Sorry, Tim, I could use you maybe; but it's impossible now." He opened the door and held it open. The boy passed into the hall and Russ and Red re-entered.

"You can guess what that was about, can't you?"

"Wants to come back? Well, nothing succeeds like success, Don."

"Sees he made a mistake. Well, it's too late now. Probably wouldn't have made the team anyhow, the way Jackson Piper is going," he said in an undertone to Russ, still bouncing the ball methodically.

From his usual place at the window, Red heard the name. "Oh, Don, Mis' Palmer asked me to tell you Jackson won't be at practice this evening. His dad telephoned the office and said he had a bad cold."

The noise of the bouncing ball stopped. From the hall outside the sound of Tim's protests came through the open door. Don looked at Russ, who was looking at him, each thinking the same thing. Jackson is sick! Jackson Piper out of the Regionals! And a likely replacement refused permission to rejoin the squad!

"You had to do it, Don, you had to do it. Boy, you can't make rules and not stick by 'em, no matter who gets hurt. Nothing else to do."

Don stepped over and took his assistant by the shoulders. He felt the warmth of the remark and the support the other was extending. But he was worried and sore. That structure which had been so carefully built was falling. Jackson sick! Tim, his best replacement and a veteran player, refused a place on the squad. Russ was right, it was the only thing to do. But . . .

"Hang it all, Red, why on earth didn't you tell me?" Ten minutes earlier and things might have been saved. Nope, I had to do it. No matter what happened to Jackson, I had to keep Tim off the squad.

"I did. I mean I forgot . . . I meant to."

He acted quickly. "John! Oh, John Little!" The group of boys surrounding Tim Baker broke up. "John, you'll go in at Jackson Piper's spot. C'mon, you guys, we got work to do this evening. Lotsa pep now, lotsa pep, c'mon everybody!"

They pounded up the stairs. Every man was on his toes. The varsity took one end of the floor, throwing baskets, throwing the ball around, warming up.

Hang it all, ten minutes sooner and I could have saved things. Nope, by George, I had to do it. I b'lieve I'd have had the courage to go through with it anyhow.

He watched John Little closely. He was six feet tall, angular, fast. Not a bad player, there were possibilities there; but he certainly lacked the catlike quickness and the lightning reflexes of the colored boy. Well, here goes!

Two short blasts on his whistle. "O.K. Let's get to work on outa bounds plays. The ball is outa bounds here. The game is tight, we're pressing 'em, and four points behind. Chuck! Move in closer to your pivot there . . . there . . . now!"

The pound-pound of feet, the quick calls of the players, the thud-thud of the ball echoed through the room. Anxiously he watched for several minutes. The boy was certainly no Jackson Piper. Maybe we'll get Jack in there for a few minutes on Saturday, after all. It probably isn't much, just a little cold. Or if not for the Regionals, for the Semifinals at Muncie. That is, supposing there are any Semifinals for us!

After a while he blew his whistle. "Wait a sec, wait a bit, Jim." The tall boy with the glasses taped to his forehead paused. "Ain't a mite of use throwing way out there. Not an earthly reason, you know that. You do? Why'd you throw then? You didn't think? Well, you gotta think. I'm holding you boys up to standards 'cause I know you can all think, every single one. John, why'd you cut in that time? You know better than that. These boys use their heads, now you use yours. Say . . . you're a good student, aren't you?"

A snicker ran round the panting circle. "Why, of course, I clean forgot. You stand at the top of the senior class. And you make a play like that! John, you oughta be ashamed of yourself. Now think, boy, think every minute of the game. O.K. Outa bounds on the other side. Sharpen 'em up a bit . . . that's it . . . sharpen 'em up a bit . . . that's better . . . don't let him run either way, Walt . . . that's good!"

Outside, the February shadows grew longer, dusk came and still they were at it, hammer and tongs, thrust and counter-thrust, reaching, shooting, racing up and down the floor. He followed them, and found himself completely tired after an hour of it. For a few minutes he permitted himself the luxury of stretching out flat on the boards of the floor behind them, his head on his fists, following every move. After a while he rose and went up into the balcony, seeing things he hadn't seen before.

"Tom! Look, Tom . . . you're wide open for that shot. A'right . . . that's more like it." He blew his whistle again. They stopped and looked up; Tom, with the crew haircut, and Walt MacDonald and Jim Turner, his eyes blinking behind his glasses, and tall, red-faced John Little and Chuck Foster. "O.K., there's a short time left in the game, say two-three minutes . . . two minutes and we're in front by a point . . . now, le's go!"

He descended to the floor. They were tired and hot; so was he. Dusk changed slowly into darkness; still he kept them at it. After a while he blew his whistle and gathered them around, their bodies steaming with perspiration, their mouths open.

"Now this man Joey Fitts . . . this kid they got over to Marion . . . he's a fifteen-sixteen point man . . . *if we let him.*" His voice rose, he barked, for he was getting hoarse. "But that's something else again; we aren't a-gonna let him. He likes to take that ball . . . oh, he's fast all right . . . he's awful fast . . . he likes to take that ball and cut for the corners, then shoot, see . . . like this."

He reached out and grabbed the ball from someone's arms. Dribbling it through them into the corner, he turned suddenly, whirled, and shot for the goal. The ball made an arc in the air. It descended through the hoop without touching the rim. A perfect shot. The panting boys stood watching, admiring his deftness and coordination. Unlike some coaches, this man could do the thing he was teaching.

"Keep your heads up. He can't do that if you keep your heads up. Walt, don't let him make that corner shot. Don't allow him to get to pitch that ball. . . . O.K."

An hour later, practice finished, he finally left the building with Russ Brainerd by the front entrance. Across the way was a glove factory whose second story windows had just been decorated. There were exactly eight windows facing the street, and each window carried a huge letter in red or blue cloth. One window was red, the next blue. They spelt the name of the team.

WILDCATS

And under the window on the brick wall of the factory were painted three words:

FITE-FITE-FITE

"Looks like this town's going mad," remarked Russ. "They haven't had a winner for so long they'll all go nuts if we get through this week. You win the Regionals and your life won't be worth living."

"I'll wait till I do. Besides, it isn't worth living right now. They were after me for tickets at five-fifteen yesterday morning. Well, that's how it is; that's being a basketball coach, I guess."

They parted at the corner. Don bought his evening paper and went into the Claymore for dinner. When he finally reached his rooming house, there was a note for him on the telephone table. "Please call Mr. Piper."

Holy smoke! I clean forgot all about Jackson Piper. What kind of a coach am I, forgetting a thing like that? Meant to call him up right after practice; but it just slipped my mind. He searched nervously through the telephone book. He dialed the number. A woman's soft voice replied.

"Mr. Piper, please."

She hesitated. "Who is this, please?"

"This is Don Henderson. The coach at the High School."

"Oh, yes. I'll call him. He's just back from the hospital, and I didn't want to disturb him unless it was important. You got his message, didn't you, this afternoon?"

"Yes." Then he added, "I only want to ask after . . ." But she had left the telephone. That word hospital had an unpleasant sound. It was some time before the anxious coach heard the gentle voice at the other end.

"Yes, Mr. Henderson?"

"I got your message, I meant to call you earlier; we had a long practice tonight. How's Jackson coming on? Is his cold bad?"

"He has pneumonia, Mr. Henderson. He's at the hospital now, and they've been giving him sulfa drugs all day."

Pneumonia! Sulfa drugs! That's the finish. That's the end. There goes the team!

8

"Mind if I sit down?"

Don, buried in the *Evening Press*, looked up with some annoyance. He did mind for he wanted to be alone. The figure at his side refused to wait for an answer but drew out the chair opposite.

"I'm probably the one man in Springfield who won't ask you for tickets to the game Saturday, so you better let me sit with you."

Don's annoyance vanished. He grinned and

folded up his newspaper. "Why, sure, Mr. Wilson, mightly glad to see you." After all, you can't be rude to a member of the School Board and, besides, Peedad Wilson interested him. There was something in the rather seedy yet fiery little man that was attractive, no matter what anyone said. Certainly as he sat there he didn't resemble a criminal much. He was just a gray-haired man with the seat of his pants almost worn through by twisting and turning in his swivel chair in that dingy office on Superior Street.

"Sit down, sit down. You don't get to come in here to the Claymore very often, do you, Mr. Wilson?"

"No, the wife's over at Earlham visiting her dad today, so I stayed late in the office and dropped in for dinner. How's the team coming along, Don? I hear fine things about your work."

"Do you? Well, we're hard at it. We could even have beaten Marion next Saturday, I think, if we hadn't lost Jackson Piper, our colored boy. He came down with pneumonia this week. Marion might win the tourney this year; they're really hot right now. But I'm not giving up on our boys; I'm not giving up on 'em yet."

"Quite right," said Peedad with emphasis.

"Never give up on the youngsters. Ask 'em, and they'll always come through for you."

Don was interested. "Why, you know, it's funny you should say that, Mr. Wilson. That's what I believe."

"Of course, of course. The more you ask, the more they'll deliver. Kids are wonderful. It's the old folks we have trouble with in this-here town." He glanced round, glaring at the room full of diners. "Well, I know you've done real good. J. Frank was praising you to the skies the other evening at the School Board meeting. That means you're in, so to speak."

Don resented that. He was a friend of the Shaws. He was getting fond of Tom the more he knew the boy, and he liked J. Frank despite what everyone said downtown. "Mr. Wilson, I've been reading your paper off and on for quite some time, now. . . ."

"That's good of you, Don."

The remark upset him. He stumbled a little. "I mean . . . I read it a good deal, and I'm wondering just what it is you've got against the Shaws. Take Tom, for instance; there's a kid with all the guts in the world, a kid who really has what it takes. Yet lotta folks hereabouts figured I put him on the team because he was J. Frank's son. Because he was a West Sider. Oh, you'd be surprised; folks said some things last year that really hurt. I put him on because he was the best player in that spot, because he's the smoothest thing off the bankboards in Howard County, as he's proving. Happens I know his dad, too, and a nicer guy never existed. Why, he's an old basketball star himself, played for Butler back in the days of Farnsworth and . . ."

"Skip it, Don. You wouldn't understand. Most probably Frank Shaw does what he thinks is right."

Don was puzzled. If a man did what he thought was right . . . "Yes, but what do you want him to do? If he does what he thinks is right."

"Do what *is* right, Don. We often act according to the way we think, but we think the way we want to. Get it?"

He really didn't. "Why, you talk as if he isn't a good citizen!"

"Well . . . I'll say this for J. Frank: he's no waster. He works hard; for a rich man's son he's a hard worker. And he hasn't chucked this town to go and live in Paris or on Michigan Boulevard or Park Avenue the way some rich men's boys do from these parts."

"And look, Mr. Wilson, Frank Shaw's on every board, every committee, everything in this town."

As he spoke he wished he hadn't said it. For there was a look in the eyes of the elder man that stopped him. It was the same half-amused glance of a teacher in high school who knows the pupil doesn't have his lesson and is trying to fake it.

"I certainly wouldn't attempt to deny that," he answered with some emphasis in his voice. There was something in his tone which dampened Don's enthusiasm. It was a warning sound, indicating that, like the high school teacher, he knew more about the subject under discussion.

Undismayed, Don continued. "Mr. Wilson, lemme tell you. Everyone in town knows the Shaws gave the hospital, and the swimming pool, and the new Y, and the memorial park, but what folks don't know is the number of times they're called on to help without it getting round. Like, I mean, when there's a deficit in the community fund or the Red Cross."

Food arrived and the other began to eat. "Let's be concrete, Don. If you are going to live in this town, and I certainly hope you are for we need young fellas like you, it's about time you knew what it's all about. The Shaws are about the only people I know who've managed to increase their personal fortune by philanthropy. Now take this matter of the municipal swimming pool. You brought it up—I didn't. Actually, most people think the Shaws gave it to the town. They didn't; they loaned half the money to the city at six per-cent interest, the other half came from you."

"From me?"

"Yes, Don, from you. It was federal money; that comes from the taxpayers of the nation; that's you, boy, and me, and all the folks in this room. Never mind, skip it. Point is, well, lemme ask you a question. And I'm wonderin' how you'll answer." He laid down his knife and fork on the edge of his plate and, leaning over, looked at the young coach. "You let colored boys play on your teams?"

"They're Americans, aren't they?" His voice was cool.

"Good! Fine! That's the kind of talk I like. Now let me ask you another. Suppose you had five boys, the best basketball players in town, no question about it. They're all colored. Would you play 'em?"

He didn't answer offhand; he thought. For Don

Henderson knew the State in which he had been born and raised. He knew this wasn't a question to be answered without thought. So he thought some time before replying. Finally he said quietly, "Mr. Wilson, I believe I would."

"Even if the Chamber of Commerce objected? If Rotary came to you and objected?"

"If they came to me, I'd listen to 'em because I'm a public servant. But I'd play those boys."

"Even if the School Board intimated to you off the record that if you did they wouldn't be able to renew your contract?"

This time his answer was not long coming. "Seems like I would, Mr. Wilson."

"Fine! Now that brings us back to the municipal swimming pool. You think colored boys are Americans. O.K., d'you think they should be allowed to swim in the pool?"

Don wasn't to be trapped so easily. "Well . . . yes . . . I mean . . . that's different. Now you take swimming . . ."

"I see. You'll go along just so far. Like everyone else in this town."

The tone made him uncomfortable again. He was annoyed. "See here, Mr. Wilson, I don't mind swimming with colored boys myself. But there's lots of folks in this town that do. They might be right; they might be wrong; anyhow, that's how they feel. In this country the majority rules; they're in the majority here in Springfield."

"Exactly. I'm coming to that. You'd admit, no doubt, that if the colored boys can't swim in the big pool in the park, they should have one of their own."

"Why, yes, I suppose so."

"Good! Most folks wouldn't go along with you. But I raised such hell on the Board they finally got round to building 'em a smaller one a couple of years ago out on the South Side. I bet you never been on the South Side since you came to town."

"You lose. I've been through there. I never saw the pool, though, I don't believe."

"D'you guess J. Frank has ever been near there?"

"I dunno."

"I do. He hasn't. Three, no, two summers ago something went wrong with the drainage and a couple of kids got typhoid. They closed the pool right away and that was that."

"You mean to say it's still closed?"

"I do. Just that, it's still closed, still full of leaves and rubbish. Go down some time and have a look. I've been fighting on the School Board all year to get an appropriation to clean it up; J. Frank has stood me off by claiming it's a job for the Recreation Commission. Of course, the Recreation Commission has no money, and he darn well knows it."

"Oh! I see. I didn't know. . . ."

"Lots of things you don't know about this city. I'm hoping you'll stay with us long enough to learn them. Too many of the good youngsters grow up here and then light out for New York or Chicago."

Don could remember he had heard the same words from Frank Shaw. Anyhow, he thought, there's one thing the two of them agree upon. The elder man continued:

"Don, as an editor I've worked all my life on two principles. They were Lincoln's principles. First, that the people deserve to be told the truth, and that if you tell them the truth they'll make the right decision every time. The second one is not very original, either; but many good Americans had to die for it in the last hundred and seventy years. If they hadn't, boy, you wouldn't be in Springfield now, coaching basketball. Here 'tis. This country belongs to the people. Not to the Frank Shaws."

Hang it all, this fiery little fellow, this small figure that Frank Shaw could crush with his fists, wasn't entirely wrong. He couldn't be; he just couldn't be.

"Reason I like you is because I found out you care for the kids. Never mind how I found out; I found out, that's enough. Don, what this town is in fifteen years depends on you. And how you handle 'em right here, now, today, in that gym. That's why I'm mighty darn glad I held out against those two fellas and insisted on you."

This was more than Don could take. "Why, Frank Shaw picked me out! He was the one who stuck to it and insisted on hiring me."

The elder man stopped him with a look.

"The facts are these. Both J. Frank and Tom Sherrill were dead against you. Not that they didn't like you personally, simply that they felt you were too young. Too young, too young, too young! I heard it at every Board meeting. So far as I'm concerned, that was a darned good reason for hiring you. We've got far too many older men in education in this town; there's enough antiquity in our school system as it is."

"Why . . . I thought . . . I understood . . . Frank Shaw gave me to believe . . ."

"I know. Now that you've panned out all right I can imagine J. Frank thinks he chose you himself, all alone. He's a former star, he knows the game, doesn't he? You're a success as a coach. He's on the Board, and that's how it goes. It's what I was saying just now; we get to think the way we want to."

"Oh! I see. I didn't understand."

"Point is everyone likes you. The boys tell me you're a hundred percent, and folks who were dead against you last year for standing up to those kids and throwing 'em off the squad, now say you're a courageous guy. Best of all, you're turning out a winning team. I can imagine what Frank Shaw says today. Never mind. But let me warn you one thing. The Shaws are fine people—until somebody disagrees with them. When you once cross 'em, watch out! If you play ball, same as everyone else in town, fine and dandy. Cross 'em, and you'll darn soon wish you hadn't. Mary!"

The waitress paused at their table and, whipping out the pad of checks tied to her waist by a string, added up Peedad's bill, and put it face down at his side. Carefully he counted out fifteen cents in nickels and, placing them beside his plate, rose.

"Must get along. Lots of work to do this evening. Good night, Don, and the best of luck to you Saturday at Marion."

Don sat alone at the table. It was the most confused moment of his life. What on earth did the old geezer mean; folks think the way they want to! Now just what did he mean by that? Something's screwy here. I never heard criminals talk the way he does. This country belongs to the people. . . .

9

". . . And, folks, this big Memorial Coliseum here at Marion is jammed, I wanna tell you, five thousand five hundred people, and not one seat, not an inch of space to be had. You know, all the wise boys have been saying the winner of the Tourney would probably come out of Marion, for this North Central Conference is really tough. But the Kats are hot, they've begun to pour it on this quarter. There goes the whistle! A jump ball in Marion territory between Little and Beckley . . . the score, Marion Giants, 20; Springfield Wildcats, 12. This whole Coliseum is going mad as the Kats start to roll. There's the jump . . . Little flips to Shaw . . . who passes to Jim Turner in the corner . . . who fakes to Little . . . who . . ."

Back in Springfield, J. Frank Shaw blew his nose violently, tossed his cigar stub into the fire, and took up a fresh one.

"Daddy, you shouldn't smoke so much with that cold of yours," said his wife.

"Gotta do it. Can't stand this. Hang it. I shoulda gone, just the same. If Don had one more good boy in there, one more star, he'd win the State. He's made a team out of 'em, a team out of nothing at all. What's that? Why, of course they're gonna beat these birds. I'm glad I held out for him." He puffed vigorously while the voice of the announcer, sixty miles distant, filled the living room.

". . . Little fouled by Lindley . . . and we'll have one free throw. They line up in the free throw zone . . . there goes the toss . . . it's no good . . . recovered by Shaw off the board . . . he passes to Mac . . . back to Shaw again . . . he's in there . . . he turns and makes a one-hand toss . . . *It's good* . . . and the score is now 20 to 14. Folks, these Wildcats are . . . they were down 17 to 6 at the start of the second quarter, but they've begun to roll now. There, Joey Fitts has the ball, Joey has the ball for Marion . . . past the ten-second line . . . to Leach . . . who shoots from way out on the floor . . . a desperate shot and . . . it's no good . . . and there's the gun! The second quarter is over. Folks . . . at the end of the first half . . . it's Marion's Giants, 20; Springfield Wildcats, 14. The Kats got hot the end of this half, and hit for eight points in those last few minutes. The way they're shooting now, it's anyone's game, anyone's."

•

Don followed the crowd pouring downstairs. They can win, he thought! Certainly they can win. Old Peedad was right; you ask it of 'em, and they'll come through.

They swarmed into the dressing room and slumped down, heads between their knees, wiping away the perspiration, panting, murmuring a word or so to the man at their side. Several stretched out flat on the hard benches. Don walked round, patting them on their shoulders, covering their wet backs with towels and sweaters. No one said much at first. Between the halves of a close game a dressing room is a tight-lipped place.

"Just relax! Relax, boys . . . stretch out, Tom, that's right. Wipe your face off there, Jim. How ya feel? Ya do? Good! You were right in there, that second quarter. O.K., John, good work; you couldn't seem to miss when you finally got your mitts on that ball. Listen, Walt, they have two on you. No more . . . no more. No more fouls, boy. Relax, fellas, just relax."

He turned aside, whipped off his coat, started to roll up his sleeves with nervous, quick hands. Save for the heavy breathing of the players, the room was silent. Red Crosby darted about, fast and active for a fat boy, handing out towels or pieces of gum to the beaten boys on the bench. Don grabbed the scorebook from Russ Brainerd and looked at it eagerly. His hands trembled as he stood there, and in order that they should not see his nerves he turned his back. One finger passed under his shirt collar from back to front, and he stretched his neck.

He turned back to them. "O.K., now." In his vest and shirt sleeves he stood before them.

Mouths open, the weary, breathless boys raised their heads. "One on Jim. One on John. Two on Tom and two on Walt. No . . . yes, that's right, two on Walter. No more . . . no more."

He leaned over and with a piece of chalk diagramed the foul circle, the foul line, and the basket on the concrete floor at their feet. "Now then. You fellas were plain scared there in that first quarter. I wanted to go in and kick you, only I knew you'd find your feet, and you did! First off, you let them run away with the ball-game. Mind you, I'm not blaming anyone; you boys aren't veterans. I understand; it was your first crack at a big place like this, and you were all a mite nervous. That's natural. As soon as you got used to conditions, you found yourselves, like I knew all the time you would." He paused and stood looking at their hot, wet faces. They can do it. They can do it, I know they can. How'll I tell 'em so they'll understand what I feel?

"Now this place is big, the crowd's big; forget it. This Marion team is good; they're supposed to win, they ain't a-gonna. Forget 'em. We're gonna knock 'em off, *if* you play your game; if you play like you did the end of this last quarter. When you got going, when you started to play

86

your game, the game I *know* you can play, you took 'em off their feet. They aren't a bit happy over in there right now. You surprised them when you began to pour it on, but you didn't surprise me, 'cause I know what you can do. I know how good you are."

Russ Brainerd at his elbow stuck four fingers before his face. Four minutes left. He nodded and squatted down over the rough diagram on the floor. "Tom! When that defense drops back and works blocks on you, when they begin ganging up around the basket, you start shooting from way out. Understand, boy? See? How far? 'Bout twenty-five feet. John, you didn't realize what they were doing, you didn't get it until almost the middle of the second quarter, and then . . ."

He reached round to the assistant coach for the scorebook. "Then you hit for . . . for how many, Russ? For three quick ones in succession. Jim, watch that Joey, watch him every second. You're a better thinker'n he is; don't let him pull that old one on you. He's coming in . . . there . . . and then cutting back, faking, and shooting from here. Get me? See, Jim?" His chalk marks did a little dance across the rude diagram on the floor. "*Don't let him.* Keep that hand up there . . . upset him . . . don't let him get that ball down."

He turned abruptly and walked around nervously. The boys, leaning over, looked at him, following him with their glances. He turned back toward them. "Don't try to jump that ball in there, Tom; you know better'n that. Wrist 'em in. Now . . ." He swung back and faced them, his legs apart. "This third quarter is the time to turn it on. You've all seen Fitts; you know he's no superman; you held him cold that last quarter. Just watch your fouls. *Watch your fouls*. Boys, I got confidence in you . . . to beat this team. Get out and go!"

The sound of clapping hands, the scuffle of feet, the noise of benches scraping on concrete, and the chorus of young voices rose over the room. Clap-clap; clap-clap. "Let's go, let's go get 'em. . . . O.K., Tom, let's go!" Towels and sweaters were tossed aside. There was an eager rush for the door to the gymnasium. To victory or defeat.

•

The roar which had filled the Shaw living room in Springfield all day rose in volume and intensity. There was a savage note in it now. J. Frank, unable to keep still, snuffling and blowing his nose, paced the floor, an unlit cigar which was ragged at the end in his mouth. He was tossing in every foul, leaning into every throw, racing up and down the court on every play. He couldn't contain himself.

"Lotsa folks mighty unhappy if he upsets this Marion bunch. Why, they were slated to go right through to the Finals at Indianapolis; yes, sir, right clean up to the Finals. The hot money's riding on Marion tonight, plenty of it. Well, I'm glad I held out for this boy, Don; he's young but he's a great coach; he's taken just an ordinary bunch of youngsters and made a great fighting team out of 'em. I always said he had it; he's young, but after all this is a young man's game."

From the davenport his wife asked, "Do you think he can do it, Dad? Oh, wouldn't it be wonderful! If only he could win this game and take the boys to Muncie next week."

"He'll win. Listen to that!"

A roar drowned out the voice of the man at the mike whose words were undistinguishable in the big living room. Little by little they began to make out what he was saying.

". . . With one minute left, folks, only sixty

seconds of this wild ballgame . . . the score is . . . Springfield Wildcats, 41; Marion Giants, 40. Folks, this is the biggest upset of the season. Absolutely! And now Springfield is hugging that ball . . . only seconds to go now . . . they pass it round the circle . . . *oh* . . . he's grabbed it . . . little Joey Fitts sneaked in there and stole that ball from Turner . . . he's off . . . he's covered . . . to Leach . . . to Beckley . . . back to Fitts . . . he shoots!"

In the living room of the Shaws the man and the woman looked at each other with despair. The frenzied shriek from the mike told the story plainly enough. It buried the announcer by its volume. An age passed before he came on again.

"Marion, 42; Springfield, 41. What a ballgame! What a game! Fifty-five seconds . . . fifty seconds . . . forty-five seconds . . . and Marion is stalling in the center . . . hullo . . . there's a wild pass . . . it's Springfield outa bounds . . . Little has it . . . a sleeper play . . . he throws down to Shaw . . . a hook shot under the basket . . . he hooks it over the top . . . *no good* . . . he follows in . . . the tall center is right in there . . . he tips it up . . . no . . . the ball rolls on the edge. . . ."

In the frenzied Coliseum the gun sounded. Its sound even penetrated the noise from the roaring stands. The scoreboard flashed once, twice, settled into:

SPRINGFIELD 43   MARION 42

Pandemonium. Confusion. Fans boiled onto the floor. A Marion supporter rushed at the Springfield bench and tangled with one of the Wildcat subs. An irate rooter struck John Little behind the ear, and immediately three members of the team jumped him simultaneously. The floor was covered with surging, milling spectators, officials, police, players. Only the Springfield contingent, deliriously happy, stayed put.

"Springfield Wildcats . . ." A thousand fists rose into the air. ". . . Clap-clap-clap." A thousand hands went together and two thousand feet stomped in unison on the boards. "Springfield Wildcats . . . clap-clap-clap. Springfield Wildcats . . . clap-clap-clap . . . Springfield Wildcats . . . clap-clap-clap . . . Yea! Wildcats! Yea! Wildcats! Yea! Wildcats!"

10

The big boy with the crew haircut opened the front door.

"Hi, coach!"

"Evening, Tom." He squeezed the great paw that was extended and touched the boy's arm. "How you feel tonight? That fall hurt you?"

"Naw."

"Hullo, Don." The host bustled forward. "How are you this evening?"

"Just fine, Frank, how are you?"

"Fine, Don, fine. Give me that hat and coat."
When he opened the hall closet, the visitor saw
a bag of golf clubs in one corner and several
tennis racquets in presses against the other corner. At this moment Mrs. Shaw appeared through
a door in the rear, and Don caught a glimpse of
the back stairs and a basketball hoop hung at
the correct height overhead. This was indeed an
athletic family.

And an athletic evening. Like all right-think-
ing citizens of Springfield, J. Frank was keenly
interested in everything which helped the town
and especially basketball. So were his friends
and their wives: Townsend Bell, a former Yale
athlete who, besides being a business friend of
J. Frank's, was a prominent banker in the cap-
ital; Jimmy Morgan, an executive of the General
Motors plant in town, was a Wildcat rooter, who
never missed a game; Harry Green, the town's
leading attorney and a well-known politician,
was a former basketball star at Indiana U.

These were important persons. All of J. Frank's
friends were important. That evening these important people were interested in one thing—
the game. You couldn't forget it. Not only had
they all read the front-page story in the morning

Tribune, but also the blow-by-blow account in the *Indianapolis Star*. The crowd in the Shaws' large living room looked curiously at Don as he was introduced.

So that's Don Henderson! Is that the great Don Henderson everyone's talking about? He doesn't seem much older than Tom Shaw!

Don, in turn, looked curiously at them. Is that really Jim Morgan that everyone at G. M. speaks about with such respect? Is that heavy figure talking to Mrs. Shaw Harry Green, *the* Harry Green who is slated to be the next mayor? Don watched them all with attention. He felt he was getting a peek at the inside of Springfield, the folks who made the city move. He sat, slightly bemused by the scene, not very happy, with a plate of food on his lap, his coffee on a small, unstable stool quite within upsetting distance of his knees.

Finally everyone finished eating. J. Frank pulled up a chair before the fire and, turning it round, sat down with his arms across the back. If anyone was uncomfortable, it wasn't J. Frank, who was enjoying himself. "Now then! Don's going to tell us the whole story from start to finish. Tell us all about it, Don; we're mighty anxious to know what really happened over there."

Chairs creaked. Someone shoved forward to hear better. The men were silent. The women looked toward Don with respect.

Great heavens, he thought, I'm famous because I've taken the Kats into the Semifinals. I'm someone to these big shots. I can't live up to this.

"I'd rather let Tom tell you. Those kids were the ones who turned the trick at Marion."

The big boy uncoiled his legs and grinned. His father, however, was not to be put off. Surrounded by his friends, he was presenting his protégé, the most talked about person in Springfield at the moment, possibly destined to be even more famous in the future. At the same time J. Frank was indirectly displaying one of his talents, a talent that was almost a genius for improving and benefiting the community. So he was in a fine humor. His tone was genial, yet firm. "Just like that! Send five kids out and they'll turn the trick. I'm an old basketball player myself; I know it ain't so. Don, it hurt to miss that game. I wanted to see Tom play the worst way. First game I've missed all winter. But the idea of plowing back sixty miles through snow and sleet with this cold was too much, even for me."

Don ran the forefinger of his left hand inside

the neck of his collar. Everyone was looking at him. "Yeah, wish you'd been there. Tom played a swell game; so did the other boys. I don't hardly know's I blame you, though; that storm was really fierce. But we had quite some fans come over, I guess. I didn't pay much attention to the crowd . . . until afterward."

J. Frank lighted a cigar. "Don! Come clean now. Did you think our boys could take that gang?"

"Why, I knew they'd come through if they played their game. 'Course, losing Jackson Piper was a tough one, but it didn't upset them, and John Little did better'n I anticipated. Everyone's been saying an' saying how Marion had the best team in years, and how they were due to go right through to the Finals. I pay no attention to the newspapers; naturally, the fans do, that's how they get their dope. So when we nosed 'em out at the finish, the home crowd was mighty disappointed and they sorta got out of hand."

"Who started it?"

"Who did start it, Tom?"

"First I saw, someone from the Marion stands rushed out on the floor and took a sock at John. So Jim and me jumped this fella, and then there must have been fifty scraps going on all over the place at once. No one's taking any socks at John while I'm around," he said firmly.

"Is it true they locked you in the dressing rooms afterwards?" asked someone.

The coach and the boy looked at each other with amusement on their faces. Don replied, "Nope! It's the other way about. They finally got us downstairs and locked the door to keep the crowd out. All the time there was two-three thousand folks milling around upstairs trying to get at us."

J. Frank removed the cigar from his mouth. "The hot money!" he said with emphasis. "The hot money was riding on Marion. Lotta gamblers there from upstate. Those people took a terrific beating last night . . . a great . . . big . . . beating."

"I wouldn't hardly know about that. The crowd was mostly older people. When they finally cleared the floor and got 'em all out of the gym, the cops had to throw a cordon around the place to keep the wild ones from smashing the windows and breaking into our dressing room."

"In all that snow! You mean to say the crowd stayed outdoors in that blizzard last night?"

Tom nodded violently. "Yes, ma'am, they sure

did. They stayed right there, hollerin' and yellin' at us and callin' us names until two o'clock. We wouldn't have got out then if we hadn't had a police escort all the way to the county line."

Someone changed the subject. It was a man, and by his question Don knew he once had been a player. "This Beckley, the Marion coach, I understand he got pretty upset. That right?"

"I understand he did. You know he had a boy on the team," answered Don. "This kid was one of the forwards; played a swell game, too. Dick Lewis of the *Tribune*, who's a friend of the old man, went to school with him over at Richmond, told me in the car coming home that Beckley practically assaulted him in the lockers afterward."

"What happened?"

"Oh, Dick told him off. Says, 'Calm down, Beckley, calm down. Looka that kid of yours out there this evening; that kid has ice-water in his veins.'"

The circle stirred, the men leaned forward. This was off-the-record stuff, something no newspaper was printing. They felt themselves on the inside of big events. They listened with attention.

Their deferential attitude made Don uncomfortable. Why, they act like I knew more about things than they do! He was confused. Because he was confused he spoke the first words that came into his head. They were words he had heard from an older man. "I reckon Marion is the same as everywhere else. The kids are O.K.; the kids are wonderful. You can always depend on them to come through. It's us older folks who . . . who are . . . who make trouble."

Something warned him to stop. An unpleasant quietness filled the room. There was a queer look in their glances. The subject was changed, quickly.

"This man, Joey Fitts. You bottled him pretty tight, didn't you?" It was Townsend Bell speaking. He leaned forward to catch the answer.

Don replied confidently. Now he was sure of himself; he was back on basketball, a subject he knew, a subject which every human being in the State of Indiana could understand. "No, no, siree; I didn't go out to play him. I never do. I never put two or three of my men on boys like Joey Fitts. See now, if a player usually scores 18 points, say, he'll score 10 or 12 points anyhow. That'll allow other men on his team to come in there and score. So I don't play for a star. He's good? O.K.; we'll give him 12 or 15 points; we'll let him grab off his 15 points, and we'll go ahead and beat him just the same."

The other man pounded one fist into the palm of his hand. He looked approvingly about the circle. "Boy, you talk sense! I saw New Albany beaten last night just that way, by putting two men on this boy Kates."

"Kates! Jerry Kates? You mean Jerry Kates of Evansville?"

"Yes. Do you know him?"

"Do I know Jerry Kates! Do I! I'll say I do. Ever since he was a little shaver so high, in grammar school. I brought him along from the time he was a kid so small he couldn't chuck a ball half the length of the floor. I taught that kid just about all the basketball he knows; on the C team, the B team, the freshman team, the varsity. He was one of my boys over at Center Township. In a small school system like that a coach is everywhere, all over the place."

"Well, I must say if you taught that boy you sure know your job. He's a sweet basketball player."

"You bet he is. How is their team? How is this Evansville club?"

"Oh, just fair. They beat Howe 38–32. They're not too hot. I doubt if they get past Washington next week."

"Mr. Henderson, do you think you'll win the Semifinals at Muncie on Saturday?" a girl asked.

Don glanced at Tom. "I hoped to win the Sectionals here. I hoped to win the Regionals at Marion. I hope to win at Muncie on Saturday," he said simply.

"Oh, I hope so!" "I sure hope so." "I hope so, too." There was conviction in every tone; they did hope so. Expressions of support and approval echoed through the room. Then suddenly the question came, the one question he had begun to dread more than anything else. It was the question he was hearing on every side, more and more.

"Don't know where we could get a coupla tickets, do you?"

He smiled. "I had almost a dozen telegrams and twice as many special delivery letters delivered to me during the afternoon. Tomorrow I'll have ten times as many waiting for me at the High School; mostly from folks I haven't seen for years or don't even know. Had a letter from a farmer, an old friend of my Dad's at home in Earlham . . ."

The pleasant voice of J. Frank Shaw boomed across the room. "I know one thing. I shall be over at Muncie on Saturday, anyhow. He's saving me four of the best, aren't you, Don?"

Luckily everyone was talking, so a direct reply was unnecessary as the big man rose and walked to the door. Don pretended he hadn't heard, but the remark made him uneasy. Hastily he spoke. "Last week someone called up at five on Sunday morning to ask for seats over to Marion. Fella that worked at the G. M. plant, one of your boys, Mr. Morgan. Said he was a taxpayer and that he was counting on me to get him two seats."

From the doorway J. Frank beckoned with a turn of his head. "Wanna show you my den. Come upstairs a second, will ya, Don?"

11

The two older men who followed him upstairs to the second floor had seen J. Frank's den more than once before. But Don was keenly interested. He looked with attention at the medals, the trophies on the long mantelpiece, the pictures on the walls of basketball teams in old-fashioned uniforms.

"This-here is the 1925 team . . . and here's the '26 team. That was my first year at center, days when we had a center jump after every goal;

boy, that was basketball, that was. And here's the freshman team at Butler, and our sophomore championship team. My junior year we beat about every team in the Big Ten we played."

"You beat us all right," said Harry Green. "That was Farnsworth's last year, wasn't it?"

"Tha's correct; Farnsworth, what a player he was! Sit down, Don, sit down in this big chair. We want to have a little talk with you. Now, boy, we really brought you up to tell you some mighty good news. We got some good news, haven't we, Jimmy? Jim is president of the Boosters' Club and . . ."

"Shucks, it was your idea, J. Frank."

"O.K., O.K. But you boys backed me up a hundred percent. Don, we're gonna put your team into the State. In fact, we're gonna cop the State for you; we're gonna fill up that gap, the gap left by Jackson Piper. Listen here, boy." He leaned over and tapped him on one knee. "How'd you like to have Jerry Kates in there playing for the Kats?"

The silence hung over the room. Don was stunned. He stammered, "Jerry Kates?" Could they mean what he thought they meant?

"Yes, Kates, from Evansville. You knowing

him and liking him and everything, that makes it just so much easier," said Harry Green.

"Y'see, Don, we figure it this way. You've shown you can coach; you've done all and more'n could be expected with these boys, with these kids you took over last year. I've been watching closely; I keep my ears open; I hear what Tom says and he knows basketball. It's my opinion the team you picked could have won the State, Don. We want to win the State."

"The Boosters' Club wants the Kats to win the State," said the prospective mayor.

"The Chamber of Commerce wants the Kats to win the State," interposed the manager of the General Motors plant.

"The whole town wants it," echoed J. Frank.

"Springfield hasn't had a winning team for years. We're determined to win this year. We're set on winning the State this winter, and I believe we can. Don, we're behind you, every one."

He was so confused by the three men, by the idea they were suggesting, by the whole situation, that he could hardly speak. "Yes . . . but Jerry's fixed down in Evansville . . ."

"Leave that to us. We've settled all that. His old man got a job in the Wire Works down there, but Jim is giving him a better job in the G. M. plant here in town."

"With Kates in there, plugging up that hole, you could win the State easy, Don. He'd fill up that gap Jackson Piper left like nobody's business; he's a mighty sweet little forward."

The sound of his voice irritated Don. "I know, I know, but wait a sec. The Principal has to certify all the players on the team to the Board of Control at Indianapolis."

"I'm on the School Board. You let me handle that Principal. Besides, Don, he'll get a better job up here, old man Kates will. You wouldn't want to stand in the way of a man's advancement, in the way of a man's getting ahead, would you?"

Don was annoyed. This remark brought him to his senses and he began to think. "Know old man Kates?" he asked briefly. "Up to the Center he was on relief all the time I was there."

The question embarrassed J. Frank. "Why, no, but I'm sure he'd like to improve himself; he wouldn't refuse a better job; a man's gotta look out for his family."

Don cut in. "If Trester at Indianapolis finds this out, if the Board of Control gets wise, they might step in and disqualify the school for a whole year."

"That man Trester better mind his business. Besides, there's nothing wrong; Jerry's dad gets a better job'n he has; he comes to town, naturally the kid goes to High School."

Jimmy Morgan tapped the end of his cigar on the firescreen. "Don, would you wanna penalize the boy? Would you wanna keep him off the team just because he's good, would you?"

"You being close friends with the boy, you having brought him along and everything, at Center Township, that makes a difference," explained J. Frank, with just a touch of anxiety in his tones.

Don regretted ever having mentioned Center Township and his coaching days there. The three men bombarded him, beat down his unexpressed objections, overpowered him with words. But the frown deepened on his forehead.

"Why, listen, Don. Over to Jackson some years ago they got four men jobs, *four men* whose sons were on the team. I know they did. I can prove it."

"And, Don, at South Bend a coupla years back they offered the coach a thousand bucks over and above his pay if he'd . . ."

This was too much. This thing had gone far enough. "Yes, I remember all that. I heard about it when I was coaching at Center Township. They gave this fella Corey four star players; he reached the Finals of the State. O.K. Where is he now? Working in a factory in Cleveland. And Jameson at South Bend isn't coaching any more, either. I want to stay in this game. I don't want to quit. What's that? Why, sure, I like to win, same as everyone. Not this way."

"Now, now, don't be hasty. Don't be hasty, Don. Take a couple of days and think it over. You'll understand how it is."

"Look, Don, you don't need to know a thing about it. The Boosters' Club will do it all. Besides, you know, we could use Kates on the Wildcats."

"Mr. Morgan, I don't really believe we need that boy. I'm not sure he'd fit into our attack. And I'm of the opinion John Little has possibilities."

"What!"

"Compared to Jerry Kates?"

"Why, he isn't in the same league."

The three older men laughed. Don stuck to his statement. "No, not at present he isn't. Give John time, give him time."

"Don, listen, boy. You want to win the State;

every coach does. You've lived for it, struggled for it, dreamed about it ever since you started to work with kids. Now with Kates in there we're a sure bet to win. This is our year."

"Mr. Morgan, I don't want a team that buys players. I'd rather take our chances. Lemme tell you they're better'n most folks think, these boys."

J. Frank Shaw interrupted. "Don, you're talking to an old varsity basketball player. For that Piper's slot, Kates is the answer to a coach's prayer. Anyhow, you think this over; just think things over until Tuesday."

"Frank, look. I picked these five kids last season when they were juniors and sophs, not one with a big name; they played the last part of the year and absorbed plenty of lickings. Now they're a unit; at last they're becoming a team; they're starting to roll. They took the punishment last year and earned their spurs, and I'd like to see 'em come through. It won't build up character to shove an outsider in there now; they'll be plenty sore."

"Character, hell! It's the State Tournament we want," said Harry Green.

"Don, you think it over and I'm sure you'll realize that with Kates in there we can go places.

Remember, you squeezed through against Marion with Little at forward, but you can't do that against the kind of opposition you'll meet at Muncie. Fort Wayne is a strong ball club this year; so is Muncie. Now you think things over for a few days."

"But I tell you now I'll feel the same way on Tuesday. If we can't win with our home town boys, let's just not win!"

An unpleasant silence fell over the room. The three older men looked at each other quickly. What kind of a bird is this Don Henderson? Most coaches would jump with joy to have a kid like Jerry Kates on their club. We try to help him, and he gives us a brush-off. Stubborn fellow, isn't he? Hard to move.

Don rose. They noticed the set of his lips and the deep frown on his forehead.

"If we can't win with the home town boys . . . if we can't . . . But, by golly, I think we can!"

12

Tom's mother rose and began emptying ash-trays into the fireplace. She went out to the kitchen carrying three or four in a pile in her hand. From the hall Tom could hear the hearty tones of his father bidding the guests good evening.

"Good night, Harry . . . good night, Jim . . . good night, Don. Now you think it over, boy . . . good night . . . good night." The front door slammed. As J. Frank came back into the room, the cars outside started and drove away. Taking a cigar from the box on the table, he reached for a match. Tom, sitting on the sofa, spoke up.

"Hey, Dad, what's all this about?"

J. Frank paused in the act of striking the match. "What about?"

"This Kates business. You been thinking about mighty little else all week, haven't you?"

He threw the match into the fireplace and an irritated look came over his face. But he controlled himself. "Tom, boy, we're gonna win the State for you. We're gonna plug up that hole Jackson Piper left."

"What hole? John's doing O.K."

"Well . . . of course . . . if you think you know more basketball than your dad . . ."

"I'm on the team, Dad."

"Look, son, do you wanna win or don't you?" The arguments with Don had not left J. Frank in the best of good humor. Now he was annoyed.

"Sure I'd like to win—with the Wildcats. Not with some kid from Center Township and Evansville, some kid that's been all over everywhere."

"Now . . . now . . . Jerry Kates is a first-class boy. I've been into all that carefully. I looked up his record. Besides, Don knows him, Don brought him along at the Township, Don likes him. Isn't that good enough? Don's a pretty keen judge of boys."

"Yeah. How does he feel about this deal?"

The elder man frowned as he looked at his boy, long legs hooked over the side of the sofa. "What makes you talk this way, Tom? Anyone would think you didn't care about basketball, that you didn't want to win. Why, Don thinks it's fine."

"I'm surprised. Myself I think it's a dirty deal. It's a mean trick, that's what; a mean trick on John Little and on the rest of us, too. On all the Kats. We came up together. Now you folks go and bust us up by throwing in a ringer."

"Ringer! Well, I like that. What do you mean, ringer? His dad's a first-class machinist. The old man got a better job in the G. M. plant here, that's all. What do you want to do, keep a man from a good job so you kids can grab all the places in the basketball team? What is this, anyhow?"

"Yeah, I know. I know what they did last year in Logansport and the year before in Washington. Logansport beat us with that Spencer kid; he scored 18 or 20 points alone. And were we sore! I know all that. Say, Dad, why don't you older folks let us kids alone?"

"Let you alone! That's a fine way to talk to your father. That's a fine thing to say when here we are trying hard to help Springfield, trying to help the team. Here we are, busiest men in town, giving time and effort, yes, and money, too, to help you boys out. And what thanks do we get? Well, that's gratitude for you!" He took a match, struck it on the brick fireplace so savagely that it broke in two. "Gratitude!" he muttered, seizing another match.

But the boy paid no attention to his words or his glaring. "I haven't talked this over with the kids. Most of 'em don't know about it yet. But as far as I'm concerned, I wish you'd leave the Wildcats alone. We're doing all right."

"Huh! Didn't do so good last year."

Now the boy was angry, too. He stood up. He towered over the tall figure of his father. "Last year isn't this year. You let us alone. We'll do O.K. by ourselves. Why do you have to try to run everything in this town? I wish you'd mind your business."

"Tom!"

She stood in the doorway with the pile of clean

ashtrays in her hand. The boy with his fists in his pocket and the elder man with the unlighted cigar clamped between his teeth were chin to chin.

"Tom! You mustn't talk like that to your father."

"Aw, Ma . . . he's always butting into things. Gee . . . I wish older folks would leave basketball alone." He turned, rushed past her, and clumped up the stairs. To the second floor, to the third floor, to his own room. The door shut with a furious bang.

13

The dressing room that next afternoon was in a feverish turmoil.

"Hey, kids, is that right!" "D'ja hear about it, Mac? Is that correct?" "Is Jerry Kates coming to school; is that so, Jim?" "We can use him all right, we can use him now." "Remember Jerry last winter on Center Township, remember how he ran around our varsity?" "Remember, Tom, remember him, Chuck?" "Oh, boy, can we go places with Jerry Kates out there! Oh, boy!"

The team, dressing in their small quarters,

was jubilant. As they yanked off their clothes and climbed into dirty practice uniforms, they were sweeping the opposition at Muncie, going on to the Finals at Indianapolis, and winning the State for Springfield. With Kates in there the Wildcats can win the State!

The squad was jubilant and excited. All except two of them. John Little, in one corner, sat silently yanking on his socks. There was bitterness in his heart. Aw, what's the use? What's the use of working and trying hard, of practicing all summer, and taking those exercises Don laid out for us, and suffering a year on the bench, and then finally earning your place, only to get shoved off for a ringer from Evansville? He's gonna move in, this boy Kates, and take over my spot.

Another member of the squad also disliked the idea. Tom Shaw's big blue eyes had a look of innocence and youth, but he was his father's son and seldom missed much that was going on around town. From the start, from the first one-sided telephone conversation he had overheard, from things he had listened to when his dad was talking to other men, he had realized what was coming before it was suggested to Don Henderson. And resented it, too.

Why should we take him? What for? We can use Kates, sure. But we're doing O.K., us kids. Why ring in this stranger on us? He's not one of the Wildcats.

Except for those two, however, everyone was excited and delighted. "With that kid we can go through the Semifinals like nobody's biz; then we'll take the Finals. We'll bring home the bacon to Springfield. Boy, with this Kates we can't miss."

Over across the hall, a more serious conversation was taking place between Don, seated on the chair yanking on his socks, and Russ Brainerd, tapping a basketball on the concrete floor.

"Boy, you're sure on a spot."

"You tellin' me," answered Don.

"This thing, this basketball, gets into people's blood. I've seen brothers fight each other about the merits of a team. Folks in this State like to win. Several years ago, over at Jackson, folks said we had to go out and get us a real coach. Get Corey, everyone said, he'll give us a winning team. But the School Board wouldn't play ball, so you know what they did? The town picked certain Councilmen, and once they were elected they chose a new School Board. And the new

Board picked Corey as coach to bring a winner to town."

"I know; I heard about it at the time. They brought Corey in. Now where is he? That's what I told those men at J. Frank's the other night." There was disgust in his voice as he finished tying his shoelaces.

"When I was at Vincennes that year, a bunch of businessmen got together in the Elks Club and went after a big-time coach. They got this fellow Hennessey, chap had a big reputation over in Ohio. You pay your expenses from the athletic fund, they told him, and you can have whatever's left. Then they brought several good players to town, made one boy's dad the janitor of the Junior High School . . ."

"Yeah. And where's Hennessey now?"

"Back in Ohio," suggested Russ, still bouncing the ball with one hand.

"I'd like to bet he's out of basketball. Thunderation, I wish I knew what to do. If I fight 'em, they'll be after me. If I don't stand up and lick 'em now, I'll be beaten in the end, no matter if we do win the State."

"That's right. Folks forget there's other years coming up," agreed his assistant.

"You bet. These birds all forget that. If you win that way once, you have to win every year. Russ, I'm determined not to string along. I told 'em so Sunday night at J. Frank's, and if they come down here bothering me, by George, I'll run 'em off the place with a pitchfork."

It was at this moment that the crew haircut and the puzzled blue eyes of Tom Shaw appeared in the doorway. Don looked up. Russ stopped bouncing the ball.

"Hi, coach. Could I see you a sec?"

"Why, sure, Tom. Come right in." Russ vanished through the door as the boy in the dirty uniform entered. Don rose and shut the door.

He came directly to the point. "Don, what about this? What do you think about all this?"

"About what, Tom?"

"Why, this bringing Jerry Kates from Evansville."

"Oh, that!"

"Sure. What do you think about it?"

"Why, how do you know? Are you sure?"

"Am I sure? Say, Dad's been talking about nothing else for ten days. He and Mr. Morgan at the G. M. plant and Mr. Green. They aim to give his old man a job at the factory and put Jerry in at forward on the Wildcats."

"H'm. I see. Well, Tom, lemme ask, what do you feel about it?"

The boy was cautious at first. "I think, well, mebbe he's overrated."

"I wouldn't wonder. How do the boys feel?"

"Oh, they want him, most of 'em. Don, who's gonna be left off the team? That's what I'd like to know."

"That's the question. Well, I'll admit I'm not so happy about it myself. Funny, I understand why your dad and Harry Green are so interested; they're both basketball players; but what's eating this man Morgan?"

The boy's eyes opened. "Don't you know? A month ago, before the Sectionals, he got a hundred bucks at 20 to 1 on the Kats to win the State. If we do, he stands to make two thousand."

"What! So that's it, betting. By golly, I won't stand it. I'll resign first. Hold on, let's see exactly how the kids feel. It's their game, after all."

He yanked open the door and stalked across the hall, followed by Tom. Inside the little room the chatter and noise ceased as he entered. He closed the door, shutting them in after the tall center came inside. Walking through to the table at the end, he stood facing the whole squad.

"Boys, you all know there's been some question of getting Kates and bringing him up here from Evansville to play on the Kats. Now what I'd like to know is how you boys feel."

Silence for a few minutes. Half an hour before the idea had excited them, but as he put it, plainly and bluntly, things seemed different. The squad looked at the floor, at their shoelaces, and said nothing. Finally Tom, leaning against the door, spoke.

"Look, you guys; this Kates is a sweet player; he's an awful good forward, so what? He isn't one of the Wildcats, is he? Of course not. He didn't get thrown in there last winter, the way we did, when the varsity quit on Don. Did he? He didn't take those lickings, night after night, same as we did all season. We took plenty. Now they want to chuck Jerry Kates in to grab someone's place, one of us who came along the tough way when things weren't too good, and folks didn't come out to the games like they do now, and the papers weren't full of the Wildcats, and . . . and . . . everything. I'm against it!"

There was a pause and then someone spoke quickly:

"Me, too."

"And me."

"Me, too."

Only red-haired John Little, whose spot Kates would fill, was silent. Then from the rear of the room a voice sounded: "Don, I'd like to ask a question. D'you think we have a chance for the State without Kates?"

"A chance? I sure do." His words came suddenly. "I sure do. You have to put out extra hard; you'd have to work like you never worked before. If you do, I believe we can go places. That's how I feel."

"What I say is . . ." Tom's words followed swiftly. "Do we really need this ringer? He isn't one of us; he's not one of the Wildcats. Let's us go out there and win or lose by ourselves; if the Kats aren't good enough to win . . ."

"That's what I say."

"Me, too."

"Hold on. Wait just a minute." Beside the table which held the blackboard Don raised his hand. "I'd like a vote on this question. You five boys on the varsity can decide it for yourselves. I'll do whatever you want. Jim, how do you feel, first?"

Every head turned toward the boy with the

glasses taped to his forehead. He blinked several times in the light. Then he spoke soberly. You could see he had been doing some thinking in the last few minutes.

"Don, I'm against it."

"Walt?"

"I'd rather stick with the gang, win or lose."

"Chuck?"

"Nuts to him . . . to this Kates."

"Tom?"

"Don, you know how I feel."

"Boys, that settles it. You've voted, you've decided; Kates is out."

Tom Shaw interrupted him. Don saw why J. Frank was a leader and a driving force in the community.

"Look, you guys! This puts it up to us, to every one of the Wildcats. We gotta do what Don says; we gotta work like we never worked before and we gotta give extra hard. We gotta put out. C'mon, gang, le's go. Le's us win the State."

The benches scraped on the concrete floor. The squad rose, yelling.

"Le's go . . . le's go . . . le's go . . . Yea! Wildcats!"

14

Thursday afternoon, and he had heard nothing from J. Frank nor done anything about the latter's suggestion either. Don, after practice, had taken a shower and dressed, save for the jacket of his suit. Across the hall came the cheerful sounds of boys enjoying themselves as only young and healthy animals can. Shouts, yells, catcalls issued from their dressing room where the team was climbing into street clothes, following their last serious workout before the

Semifinals. The practice had been long and spirited. The boys were really taking hold and Don felt happy. The Wildcats were going places.

"Sounds like they're loose," remarked Russ, his eyes on the ball he was bouncing with one hand against the concrete floor.

"Sounds like."

"Good sign."

"Yeah, basketball's gotta be fun. It's *gotta* be fun. I must get that across to these kids else they'll tighten up." He glanced round for his coat as Dick Lewis, the sports editor of the *Tribune*, came in briskly, a newspaper under one arm.

"Hi, Don! Hi, there, Russ! Hullo, Red," said Dick, speaking last to Red Crosby, the student manager. The fat boy at the window was handing out oranges and vitamin pills to the members of the squad. "Say! How about this Kates job?"

"What Kates job?"

"Jerry Kates. I'd like to get things straight. Is he coming to town or isn't he? Some of the boys in the Lions Club told me yesterday it was all set to bring him up from Evansville, but the Principal says this morning there's nothing to it. Who's correct on this, anyhow?"

"The Principal," Don said curtly. "Le's see your paper, Dick." He changed the subject.

"It's the *Muncie Press*." He unfolded the newspaper and held it out for them to see. The three gathered round his shoulders, looking with attention at a double-page spread with action pictures of the Burris team and its coach. In big letters across the page were headlines.

"LET'S GO, BURRIS

All of Muncie is Backing You. Get Set to Win Saturday. 50,000 Muncie Fans Can't Be Wrong. On to Indianapolis."

"LET'S HAVE THE STATE. BEST WISHES TO SCOTT HARRIS AND ALL OF THE BURRIS OWLS."

Underneath were the names of the hundred business firms in town who had sponsored the advertisement and paid for it.

"Ain't that something?" said Dick, admiration in his tone.

"Say! That's really something!" said Red Crosby, on tiptoes, looking over Dick's shoulder.

"They sure know how to back their team over there," suggested Russ.

Don grasped the paper. "Shoot! I'm glad they aren't playing up our kids this way. I'm having a hard enough time keeping 'em normal as it is." He turned to the sports pages.

"Burris Owls Strong Favorites to Go Through. Fort Wayne Central Picked to Beat Decatur in Opener." Underneath was the story by the sportswriter for the *Press:*

"The largest crowd of the state's four Semifinal crowds, a jam-packed capacity of 7,475, will see Central of Fort Wayne engage Decatur at 1:30 P.M. on Saturday, and Burris of Muncie tackle Springfield at 3:00 P.M. Winners will clash at 8:00 o'clock for the right to represent this area in the State Finals at Indianapolis a week from Saturday.

"Three of the contending teams were slated to be here; but Springfield was supposed to have died off along the trail. Many dopesters believe the meet will be won and lost in the evening when Fort Wayne is expected to tangle with Burris. This startling Burris team hopes to become the first to win the State crown; but Coach Harris makes no secret of his fear of the Wildcats. They displayed a strong defense against the Marion Giants; but it is not generally believed they can stop the tall Burris forward line which averages over six feet four. All tickets have been sold long ago, and Principal R. D. Shafer of Muncie Central, Tourney manager, has announced there will be no public sale. The Tournament will be covered by 68 newspaper and press association representatives, and four radio stations, including WLBC of Muncie, WOWO of Fort Wayne, WKBY of Richmond, and WSWP of Springfield."

"Here!" Don crumpled the newspaper and threw it under the bench. "Don't let the boys see this. They've got plenty to worry about as it is!" He picked up a basketball and stepped across the hall into the players' dressing room, closing the door behind him.

"Now, boys!" The squad stopped their horse-play and noise. They were dressed, some in leather jackets or sports coats with shirts open at the neck; one or two had on blue Springfield sweaters, and most wore plaid-checked caps with long peaked visors and flaps that buttoned on top. They pulled the two benches round to make a V before the blackboard and sat down, waiting, while he stood before them.

One finger went nervously inside the collar of his shirt. He passed the ball from hand to hand. "Now, boys. Basketball's gotta be fun. It's *gotta* be fun. If it isn't fun, it's no good. I want you all to have some fun for yourselves over at Muncie on Saturday. These two teams are both good; O.K., you're good, too; you proved that last Saturday night. And the way you've taken hold this week encourages me plenty. If they're good, why, we'll just go out and knock 'em off."

The ball shifted from one palm to the other. He hesitated, looking at their upturned faces, at John's serious expression, at Jim, blinking behind his glasses, at Chuck's earnest face, at Tom's crew haircut. "This game is no different from any ballgame, not a mite different. Just a few more people, that's all. You know their numbers, don't you? O.K., now, remember one thing—you cannot shoot stiff-fingered. Relax. Roll that old ball round in your hands . . . like this . . . don't get excited and chuck it any old way. Lay it . . . lay it . . . lay it . . . like you gotta egg up there you don't wanna break." He extended the ball from his chest, holding it up at arm's length. "Like that!" He walked across the narrow space between the benches and the blackboard. Easy to see who was the tightest, most nervous person in the room.

"Tom!" The word shot out. "Tom! You gotta be a smart captain out there, a smart captain. You gotta call time . . . you gotta watch . . . be relaxed. Remember, this game's like any other; just a few more people watching, that's all. That's the only difference." Again he rolled the ball in his hands, again he stepped quickly back and forth in the tiny space before the boys. His curly hair hung in two damp cowlicks on each side of his forehead. The V-shaped crease between his eyes was deep now; he was thinking hard, trying to remember everything the scouts had told him, to give them every single bit of information which would help. As Peedad said, "Tell 'em what you want, and the kids'll come through for you."

"Some teams go over to Muncie tomorrow to practice and stay all night. We don't. One basketball court is the same as any other; it's only the crowd that changes. Judging by the gang after me this week for tickets, we'll have a-plenty of rooters on those benches in the Field House on Saturday. You won't be forgotten; no, siree. Just a short drill tomorrow, just enough to limber up. I want you to have lunch on Saturday at

11:30. That doesn't mean 11:40 or 11:35, either. We play the second game, so we'll meet here and drive over at 12:30. No milk. Eat a big breakfast; remember, it's that you'll play on Saturday; not your lunch but your breakfast. Yes, Chuck, bacon and eggs . . . no cakes, no wheatcakes . . . save those for Sunday morning. Don't forget, you fellas, no milk. No milk before games; as much as you like after. No milkshakes, either. Tom, you got me, didn't ya? O.K., any questions? . . . That's all."

There was a moment of silence and then the benches banged and scraped on the concrete floor. Shouting, clapping their hands, yelling, they rushed out the door and stomped up the stairs to the exits onto the street.

Wish to goodness I was as loose as they are, thought Don. They're going to play; they'll carry the responsibility; yet they're taking it in their stride. And here I am, haven't eaten a decent meal all week!

"Hey, Don!" Russ poked his round face inside the door. "A gentleman to see you!" There stood J. Frank Shaw. He seemed out of place in an elaborate ulster with a blue silk polka-dotted muffler around his neck. The bare concrete hall made a queer setting for his elegant figure. Don's face betrayed some surprise and no great amount of pleasure. The elder man noticed the expression.

"Don, I must apologize for coming down here like this at a time when you have so much on your mind."

"That's O.K., Frank. C'mon in, c'mon in here, please." He shook hands and led him across the hall. "Frank, you know Russ Brainerd, the football coach and my assistant, and this is Red Crosby, the student manager; we wouldn't be able to run this show without Red, would we, Russ?"

"No, sir! We really wouldn't!" Red, in his blue sweater with the big S upon it, blushed furiously and hung his head as he extended a limp paw to the great man. The great man was agreeable and affable to everyone. He asked a question or two about the team, and then Russ picked up his coat and edged toward the door. He gave a commanding nod to Red, who followed him into the hall.

Don stood leaning against the bench, his fingers tightly grasping the edge. J. Frank, with a gesture, unbuttoned his coat and threw open the blue silk muffler. He stood looking about the room. Don suddenly noticed the crumpled newspaper at his feet and realized that Red had forgotten to sweep the place out during the afternoon; that the pipes showed bare above the shelves and that there were cobwebs in the corners; that there was a pungent smell from a heap of dirty towels in one corner and a pile of ancient uniforms at the end of the bench. The room was small; it was dirty; it was unattractive.

Yet J. Frank looked about with approval. He took a deep breath. He slowly shook his head.

"Same kinda place, same smells, same feeling. Doesn't change much over the years, does it? I'm like an old war horse when I get into a locker room again." He looked around. "Gosh, I envy you, Don, I envy you." It was evident he meant it. "Golly, I wish I was twenty years younger. I really lived in those days. I wish I could go through it all again."

Don felt the intensity of his words and immediately understood the other's nostalgic craving for his youth, for basketball, but most of all for one place where he was on his own. Where he wasn't J. Frank Shaw of Springfield, but No. 44, a candidate for the team, winning a spot because of his ability alone. Not because he was born in the big white house on the river but because he had something, because he was better than the next man.

Don never again liked Frank Shaw as much as he did at that moment. He began to appreciate things about him, realized how he was reliving his own youth and experiences through Tom, saw why he wanted intensely to win. For a few seconds he forgave him his errand; for a minute he sympathized with the big chap who stood looking round at the scene where he had been most completely on his own.

Then the elder man spoke and the spell cracked. "Don, boy . . . I'm sorry to have bothered you; but we haven't got your answer yet about young Kates. Now we're all set to go on this, just waiting word from you."

"Frank, I haven't changed my mind."

"Wait a minute, just hear our proposition. The Boosters' Club has thought this all out. With Kates in there we can go places, and the Board is ready to make a contract with you by which you get two percent of the gate receipts next year."

"No, thanks."

Few people in Springfield said no to J. Frank. He was not accustomed to the sound of the word. The warm, pleasant look vanished from his face.

"I b'lieve we can go places without Kates. Anyhow, we'll try."

"That's your answer?"

"That's my answer."

"Don, I'm older'n you are. I think you're making a mistake. Springfield isn't a big town; but there's a spirit of cooperation here; folks help each other out and we like people who do, who . . ."

Don interrupted. J. Frank wasn't used to interruptions, either. "Sorry, Frank, I can't go along on this. But even if I wanted to, the boys wouldn't let me. We talked it all over and held a vote on it. They voted on it and they're against the idea."

"The boys! The boys! What do they know! What have they got to do with it?"

"It's their game, isn't it?"

"The boys! At their age, how can they know what's best?"

"And that settles it."

J. Frank had a dozen things he wanted to say; they almost burst from his lips. Yet, somehow, he contained himself and finally nodded. He nodded politely, but Don had never seen such frigid politeness. Then he started to button his overcoat. With deliberation he fastened the front, adjusted the muffler, and moved toward the door. Then he hesitated. "O.K. Just as you wish. You're running the team; it's your show. By the way, Don, I need four seats for Saturday . . . could you see your way . . . if you could manage . . ."

Quite evidently the man was unaccustomed to asking favors. He did it clumsily. Don's sympathy vanished. Hang it all, this was putting him on the spot. A Thursday practice was always grim; it was long and strenuous; he had to ride herd on the boys pretty hard. Moreover, he was tired. In the ordinary way, he might have been conciliatory, have explained tactfully that the thing was impossible.

That evening, unfortunately, he was in no conciliatory mood. This is basketball; here everyone's on their own. No one gets any breaks; they earn what they get. So he spoke to J. Frank exactly as he had spoken to the man on the early shift in the G. M. plant. He stopped the man who owned Springfield just as cold as the man on the telephone that Sunday morning.

"Sorry, but I don't aim to get tickets for anyone, Frank. It's a hard and fast rule of mine."

The elder man started. He was not used to a

brush-off of this sort. In fact, he was not used to brush-offs of any kind. They were something foreign to his way of life. Yet he kept himself in hand, and replied courteously, "Well, do you think you could manage two for me? Two would help lots." He glanced expectantly.

Don wavered. I daresay I could; yes, I suppose I could. No, by George, I've kept out of this ticket mess all year and I don't intend to make an exception this late in the day.

"Why, Frank, I'd like to. But I've refused tickets to everyone all season, and I don't hardly see how I can break my rule now. If I did, I'd be sunk. You'll understand, I'm sure."

The big fellow moved through the door. "Why, that's all right, Don; I quite understand. Good luck to you over there on Saturday. I guess you'll need it."

15

They reached the big brick Field House just before the first game of the afternoon. Hundreds of cars decorated with ribbons, streamers, and colored flags surrounded the enclosure, gleaming in the bright sunshine. Boys and girls were pouring inside. The girls carried paper tassels on the ends of sticks. A knot of players in yellow satin jackets came past; members of teams defeated in the Regionals the week before, come to town to see the fun. In the crowded entrance hall the throng gave way, watching the Wildcats pass through, with Red, a couple of duffle bags over his shoulders, bringing up the rear. Hands reached out, greetings were shouted as they went down below. "There's Tom! Hey, Tom! There's Walt . . . there's Chuck! Hey there, Chuck!"

The dressing room was more commodious than the one to which they were accustomed, with lockers and benches on one side and showers over against the opposite wall. They climbed slowly and carefully into their clothes, leaned over and laced their shoes. Don walked nervously up and down.

"Red! Pop up there and find out how much time is left." The fat boy, grinning, rushed up the stairs. On a table in the center Doc Showalter was binding Walt MacDonald's weak ankle. Don walked across.

"Howsa feel, Walt?"

"Fine." The boy nodded. His eyes were wider than usual, but he was outwardly calm and composed.

Don turned away. I sure hope so, he thought. There just isn't anyone to replace him—or the others, either!

"All right now, boys." He leaned over and drew the conventional diagram on the concrete floor and, taking off his coat, stood facing them. They gathered around the benches, jaws moving in unison. Red Crosby came bounding down the stairs.

"Four minutes left. Fort Wayne, 32–26."

"O.K. Now we won't have much time up there. Just go in and shoot some baskets for two-three minutes. Start pitching free throws and take some long shots. Throw mebbe four or five on each side." The boys, leaning over their knees on the bench, watched him closely. Several were standing up behind, hands on hips, chewing violently. His voice rose.

"Start right and you'll finish right! Start right and you'll finish right! Let's *us* set the pace, let's *us* move. Move out there in front, Tom; get out there in front right away. Worry 'em. They like to come in, but they might try to throw that long one any time. Keep your hands up on the ball. When you get a sign from me, remember, go get 'em. Sleep with 'em, eat with 'em, stay with 'em. . . .

"One thing more. You're in that ballgame alla time. Not 30 minutes . . . nor 31 minutes . . .

but 32 minutes. See you don't forget it. O.K.,
then, le's go!"

"Yea! Wildcats! Le's go." They pounded their
way up the stairs, passing the victorious Fort
Wayne team just coming down to the showers.
Then through the doors onto the floor. The intense heat generated by five thousand five hundred
bodies struck them full in their faces. The noise
from the crowd as they trotted out was deafening.
En masse the stands to the right rose.

"Yea . . . Wildcats . . . yea . . . Wildcats . . . yea . . . Wildcats, fight-team-fight!"

When Don came up several minutes later to
squeeze into his place on the bench, the loudspeaker was giving the line-ups. Across the room,
the clatter from half a hundred typewriters punc-
tuated the rare intervals when the crowd roar
subsided slightly; at his right, along a wooden
desk, were half a dozen microphones with their
high priests in attendance. And above and around,
up into the dimness of the rafters, was the great
crowd, restless, noisy, eager and anxious for the
conflict to come.

And directly opposite, in the front row of the
Muncie side, was J. Frank in his big ulster,
surrounded by a party of friends.

"And here are the starting line-ups. For

Springfield . . . MacDonald, number 4, guard."
There was a huge roar after every name. "Shaw,
number 5, at center. Little, number 11, forward."

He turned quickly to watch those familiar figures twisting and turning under the basket. Then
his gaze went toward the other end at the giant
Burris squad. If only we were better fixed for
subs, they could do it. Doggone, they'll do it
anyhow. Ask the kids, and they'll always come
through.

"A number of hats and coats have been turned
in," droned the loudspeaker. "They await their
owners at the broadcasting table in the center
of the floor."

The roar subsided, rose again, died away. The
loudspeaker began the pledge to the flag, and
everyone stood.

"One nation—indivisible—with Liberty and
Justice for all." He hardly heard the words. Then
the whistle blew from the floor. The boys came
over toward him near the sidelines and gripped
hands. He leaned over with them; his boys, his
team.

"O.K., you can do it. Go out there and knock
'em off!"

They rushed to their places. The noise became

louder, louder. It never stopped completely for the twenty minutes the half lasted.

Don sat motionless on the bench, a rolled scorecard tight against his lips as usual. Silently he watched the drama unfold before his eyes. It was drama to him, more so than to anyone else in the huge enclosure. Because they were his; he knew them all, their strength and their weaknesses; he had taught them, lived with them through defeat and disaster, had seen them grow strong and reliant. And he loved every one of them and wanted them to win.

Above, the stands shrieked, rocked and roared with emotion. The Burris tactics were evident immediately. Their aim was to upset the Wildcats by passing the ball around among themselves, waiting for a chance to work inside, meanwhile slowing the tempo as much as possible and breaking up the fast Springfield game by hugging the ball.

Nuts! Whad' I tell 'em? Against this ballclub the last thing to do is hold up. Move, you guys, move! Make them move! Follow up there, Tom . . . atta boy . . . now go.

The lead shifted, alternated from side to side, first one team ahead by two points, then caught and passed by the other. It was 4–all, 6–all, 8–6 Springfield, as the first quarter ended. The boys stood in a circle in the middle of the floor, panting and talking it over, their arms on each other's shoulders, while Red shoved out the towel box. Don could see the slow Muncie offense had them rattled.

Alone, Tom Shaw was keeping them in the game. The tall center was taking the ball off the defensive backboard, ruining the Muncie tip-in game, and forcing the Owls to shoot from way out. They didn't like those long shots. Yet neither did the Wildcats like the delayed tempo, with play slowed down, with the ball held by their opponents and passed back and forth continually from man to man around the circle. They wanted to run; to get out and go. Halfway through the second period, Burris caged a lucky one, and followed that by two free throws to lead, 14–12. They were 16–14 when a foul called on Little made them 17–14 with only a minute left in the half.

Instantly Tom on the floor called time out. They clustered round him, Jim's face red and damp, perspiration running down Walt's neck, Chuck panting in his ear. Tom realized the danger as he spoke. "Look, you guys . . . we can lose this right here! We gotta grab us one bucket before the half. I'll tip the jump to you, John. Now le's go . . . get it . . . to John. . . ."

The umpire threw up the ball, and with a desperate leap Tom jumped higher than his rival, touched the ball and deflected it toward the waiting John. Now then . . . to Chuck . . . to Jim . . . to John again . . . they came down the floor. His man was closely watching him, darting back and forth with every move. He feinted desperately, stabbed in one direction, cut in, dodged a defensive player, and caught John's throw directly under the basket. He reached up and laid the ball on the edge with one hand, just as the whistle blew.

17–16. Anyone's game!

Downstairs, the five exhausted boys threw themselves on the bench. One or two rose to go over to the drinking fountain and swab out their mouths. Don followed the squad into the coolness of the dressing room, yanking off his coat as he descended the stairs. He walked around, patting each heaving shoulder.

Russ Brainerd stood with the scoreboard in his hand, a solemn-faced figure. Don rolled up his sleeves. "Relax there, boys, relax. Relax.

Get Mac a towel, Red. Wipe your face off, John."
He reached over and pulled a sweater around
Chuck's wet arms and shoulders. "Here! Lemme
see that scorebook." He stood engrossed in the
figures, while the team sat with their heads over,
puffing, their necks and backs and shirts soaked
with sweat. Gradually breath returned; one or
two heads came up, someone muttered a few
words.

"I missed that set-up in there." "No matter."
"Nor I didn't get those buckets I shoulda." Tom
spoke up. "Never mind. This time we will."

Don read from the scorebook in his hand.
"Two on Mac, one on Tom. Walt, two on you;
watch that there . . . and two on John. Now, we
haven't moved that ball like we're capable of.
D'you think so, Tom? D'you, John? Do you? No!
I told you to set the pace; you let them set it.
Move that ball. Whatever you do, move it. When
that man's open, give it to him. Pull out from
that basket; beat 'em to it. Tom, you get the ball;
you're boss . . . start moving into the front end.
Understand? We gotta go this time. We gotta
spot 'em up and spot 'em fast. One thing; watch
for the man with the ball and watch for the chance
to return it to him."

He took two steps forward and placed one

hand on John Little's sandy mop. The boy's head came up. There was affection in the look they exchanged and understanding. Slowly he spoke. "Don't foul out there, boy, don't foul."

"I didn't foul!" The answer was instant. "I didn't."

"Yes, you did."

"No, honest, Don, I didn't."

"John, I saw you hook that man there."

"Well, why didn't he call a foul on Joe Brown that time there? I didn't foul. . . ."

He replied wearily. "I expect you did, though. Anyhow, they're running this ballgame. O.K. One more thing. We're right on their tails now; but the crisis in this game hasn't come yet. When it does come, Tom, I'll give you the sign. When you get the sign from me, *go*. Pour it on. All right, pass and cut, pass and cut; le's go this quarter . . . le's go!"

Up in the arena the loudspeaker was giving the scores of the other games over the state, as well as various incidental announcements. "Bedford, 46; Washington, 30. Bedford Stone-cutters, 46; Washington Hatchets, 30." There was a slight pause. Then: "Will Mrs. Riley Heaton please call operator 42 at Crawfordsville.

Mrs. Riley Heaton, please call operator 42 at Crawfordsville. In the first game here, as you know, the Fort Wayne Tigers defeated the Decatur Yellow Jackets, 39 to 26. Fort Wayne Central, 39; Decatur, 26."

A little red-eyed man in the Muncie section rose, climbed down through the crowd, walked directly past J. Frank and his party in the front row, and went out the exit to the halls. He wormed through the people standing around and went over to a telephone booth. Finally he got into one and called a number.

"That you, Joey? Hey, Joey. Two grand on the Wildcats; even. Yeah, I said the Wildcats; Springfield. Uhuh. And they'll win tonight, too. It's Springfield by six points; even money. Burris by four, one to three. Get it? Yeah . . . yeah." He rang off and went back through the crowded hallways where all talk was of basketball, of games past, games present, and games to come.

"Them fellas from Springfield was really chucking that ball around," said a voice. Another man, as he brushed past, said, "Anyone know how the rest of the games came out?" "I do. Anderson beat Waynetown, and La Porte beat the Frankfort Dogs." "Say, you know those

Bearcats tried the darndest three-man defense I ever saw." "Well, they were too tough, I guess; that's about the size of it. Hey, there go the teams!"

Inside the arena the noise was tremendous. Cheers from both sides of the floor echoed back and forth. "Springfield Wildcats, clap-clap-clap. Springfield Wildcats, clap-clap-clap." Two thousand arms went into the air as one. Two thousand pairs of hands came together with a single great smack. Two thousand pairs of feet stomped in unison upon the boards. And two thousand voices from the Springfield side of the stands greeted their champions.

"Yea! Wildcats! Yea! Wildcats!"

The teams were coming onto the court as the little red-eyed man passed before the front row to climb to his seat. He went directly before J. Frank, who watched him go by with interest. The elegant ulster leaned over Mrs. Shaw to the friend at her side.

"Sam! D'ja see that? Henry Sweeney, the town's chief gambler. How did he get up there right behind us, anyway? Who gave him that seat, that's what I'd like to know. Beats me, how a man of that kind can grab off a place in the middle of the stands, while I find it impossible to get seats legitimately at home and hafta come over here and buy 'em from a speculator. Don't it beat all?"

He leaned back in his place. "What we need in Springfield is a coach who knows his business," he grumbled.

"But, Dad!" Mrs. Shaw turned on him. "I thought you said Don was a wonderful coach. You've been saying that all season, Dad."

The roars increased as the referee stood in the center of the floor with the ball in his finger-tips, waiting for the toss. J. Frank, watching, paid no attention to his wife. Maybe, in the noise, he didn't hear her question.

For the first few minutes of that fateful third quarter, Springfield threw up a tight defense which the Owls couldn't penetrate. Neither could the Wildcats hold the ball long enough to get in and score. After several minutes, without a point won by either side and the tension growing fast, a Muncie forward suddenly broke away from his guard and pivoted in to hit one and score. 19–16.

Instantly Don realized this was the turning point of the game. One more Burris basket would give them a five point lead, and probably an unbeatable one at this period of the contest. On the next few minutes hinged the whole battle. Springfield quickly called time; for Tom, on the floor, realized the danger also. He glanced nervously toward the bench. Don gave him the sign.

This was the moment. Go!

Arms on each other's wet shoulders, they stood there while Tom shook one big fist in their faces. "Now, you guys, let's move! Let's put that pressure on. Jim! Chuck! Walt! John! We gotta move! We gotta put out now, this is the time to pour it on."

"Le's go!" "Le's go, gang!" "Le's go!"

They went from the jump. Once again Tom tipped it to John, who rushed down and was fouled in the act of shooting by a Burris player. He made both baskets amid roars from the stands, and the score was 19–18. Burris took the ball in, came down the floor, passing it round in Springfield territory, waiting and seeking the chance to slip under the basket. Tom was here, there, on his toes, hands up, his big body beautifully balanced, ready to jump any direction, his eyes on the ball every second. A Muncie forward made a sudden flip pass to a teammate.

The other man had his back turned at that exact moment, and the ball bounced off his shoulder right into the arms of the alert Tom, who made a fast break down the floor. He hooked it up and scored unassisted. Springfield was ahead by a point.

Now the Wildcats were hot. They rallied round Tom as he reached up a moment later with a tremendous leap and grabbed the ball off the defensive backboard. Together the boys raced along the floor. To John; to Walt; over to Jim; back to Tom; to John again, who cut round a block and set sail for the basket. He passed to Walter whose try was good, and the score was 22–19. The stands seethed and rocked as the ball fell through.

Tom slapped them on the back, every one. An instant later, Jim stole the ball, ran down and, shooting from way out, caged a beauty, making it 24–19. Burris came back with a free throw; but John Little scored on a double foul and it was 26–20. Subs rushed in from the Muncie bench as the teams went into the final quarter.

Tom wiped his forehead and glanced at the electric scoreboard. There's time yet; there's eight minutes left and anything can happen in eight minutes. Six points isn't any lead at all in eight minutes. C'mon, you Wildcats.

With envy he watched fresh boys come in from the opposite side. If only we had a few good subs right now; if Jackson Piper were in here fighting with us. We could sure use Jackson here. These kids are nearly finished. They have sand in their pants now. But I'll hold 'em together, I'll pull 'em through.

"C'mon, Wildcats! C'mon, you Kats, c'mon." Desperately he slapped them on the back, John and Jim and Walt and Chuck. "C'mon now, we gotta move!"

The Burris fans knew they were tired. So did their coach; so did the stands. So did the Burris team, roaring in to cut down the Wildcat lead in those last minutes of play. Now it was Springfield's turn to hug the ball, to play a cagey, defensive game, to stall and pass it round the circle and prevent Burris from scoring. Fouls were called on both sides, missed and made; the score mounted and still Tom held the Wildcats to that tenuous lead. Despite the height of the Burris forward line, he was a tower of strength under each basket, coming up with the rebounds time and again, roaring desperately into the air when the ball bounced off the board to grab it in flight. The crowd was in a frenzy as the seconds ticked away, as the Burris team, regaining their composure, swarmed in to overwhelm the tired Kats.

"Hey . . . look out . . . cover, Walt . . . cover . . . get 'at ball . . . get 'at ball, there . . . hi, Chuck . . . hey, John!" He called his commands and they obeyed him, hearing his voice above the pounding of feet, the sharp cries of the other team, and the roar from the sidelines. "Cover up . . . watch it, Walt!" And off they went, with Burris racing for the goal. Once again he flung himself up and rose into the air, snatching the ball off the board. He came down the sidelines slowly, trying hard to catch his breath, to conserve his strength, hearing suddenly his father's familiar tones.

"Say there, Lester, say!" Dad was shouting at the referee. "They pushed him in the back! Great Scott! Letting 'em get away with that!"

Then Tom was past, the words died away, and those ever-reaching arms were before him as he tried to pass. He threw it to John who tossed it over to Jim, while Tom took a quick glance at the scoreboard as he had done a hundred times in the last half, watching time ebb slowly, so slowly. It was the last three minutes, when you lead 32 to 28, the longest three minutes of a lifetime.

A foul was called, and Walt MacDonald stepped up to make a free try. He wiped the sweat from his forehead, took the ball, bounced it twice, and looked up. From the free throw lane Tom stood poised. The ball swished through the net, and he could almost hear Walt's sigh of relief as it went in.

Now, then, they can't catch us. Surely they can't catch us now. There's only a few seconds left. Only a few seconds to go; they can't catch us unless we go to pieces. We won't either, not this gang won't. C'mon, Wildcats.

The gun sounded. The game was over.

16

In the lobby of the Roberts, a huge crowd milled around; boys from the losing teams in satin jackets; officials and former players from the region; relatives of the four contending squads; fans and friends and the miscellaneous mob attracted by a Tourney Semifinal. The floor of the hotel was so jammed you could hardly work your way through to the desk. In the mezzanine, overlooking the packed lobby, more people stood about, hanging over the balcony railing to search for acquaintances or watch the sight below. The clock above the clerk's desk showed 5:15, yet already a knot of people were gathered outside the closed doors of the dining room. It takes time to get a meal served on the evening of the Semifinals, and folk in Indiana do not arrive late at basketball games if they can avoid it.

The doors to the dining room opened. Not, however, to let the eager crowd in, but to let diners out. The Springfield team had eaten a sketchy luncheon at 11:30 that morning, and at 4:30 following the contest were quite ready for food again. The circle outside parted to permit them to come through, one or two parents saying a word as they passed. The boys went across the lobby and over to the elevators, which took them up to specially reserved rooms where they could lie down until time to depart for the Field House.

A Springfield rooter in the balcony saw them picking their way through the crowd below.

"Yea! Wildcats! Yea! Wildcats!"

On the floor people glanced up, amused at the excited, bald-headed man above. They shouted something and he instantly replied. In fact he did more than talk. He whipped out his pocketbook and yanked a bill from it, waving the bill at his hecklers on the floor.

"A hundred even! A hundred even! A hundred says the Wildcats. Anyone cover?"

A dozen voices instantly yelled from the floor. Someone bounded up to the mezzanine to take the bet.

Upstairs, the boys were soon stretched out in bed in separate rooms, resting for the battle to come. But in 1228, three men connected with the team were working hard. The Wildcat brain trust, Don, Russ, and Chester Herd, the scout, sat around a table, going over the latter's notes made on the Fort Wayne five.

"They often play a center blockout. Like this, see." He sketched a hasty diagram on a sheet of paper. "Then they turn to come outside, hoping you'll cut. Don't do it. Tell the boys they fake an awful lot, especially this Benson. But he seldom passes. What's that? Sure he's fast; he's plenty fast, but not as fast as Tom Shaw. Say, has that kid come on! First time I've seen him for weeks, this afternoon. Y'know, Don, folks in town thought last year you put him in there 'cause he was J. Frank's son. They found different, didn't they? Now this boy, Chambers, he's really as good as Benson in my opinion. Against Logansport in early February he was really better most of the time. You gotta hold your position on him; don't let him knife you, don't let him go.

"Ramsay? You remember Ramsay; we had him against us last year. He drives around on an outside block; shoots close. Gardiner comes in for Benson; not quite so shifty, not quite so fast. They use a slow offense an awful lot, like Burris tried this afternoon."

"When they saw how we took hold of things in that third quarter, they won't play any slow offense tonight. Murray's much too smart for that. They'll go from the whistle."

"Most likely. Now they want to get three on two or two on one whenever they can . . . they play for a fast break. . . ."

•

The living room of the house in Westwood where the Shaws were dining with Muncie friends was much like their own room in Springfield. There was every reason why it had the same white walls, the same fireplace in the center, the same kind of davenport, chairs, and pictures. It looked like a hundred similar rooms in similar homes, all tinged with the personality of Mary Vane, the fashionable interior decorator of the region. While the two contending teams were resting in the Roberts and the coaching staffs were hard at work preparing for the battle ahead, this room was filled with people enjoying themselves. Filled also with noise and laughter. Drinks were in evidence, and certainly the visitors at least were cheerful. Their team had won unexpectedly; might even with luck get into the Finals. They had reason to be hilarious and they were.

J. Frank, with a drink in his hand, was giving his reactions to the contest ahead. People had a habit of listening whenever he spoke; when he talked about basketball, on which he was an authority, people really listened.

"What I said at the start of the season, the boy's an experiment; just an experiment, that's all. And anything we took after the opening game of the Sectionals was so much gravy."

"He isn't deep in subs, is he?" suggested a voice tentatively.

"Deep? Hasn't got any! Not a one worth the name. That's exactly what I've been saying; a good coach builds up a squad, not five players. But it's his own fault. F'rinstance, he tossed Fred Rogers' kid off, and he was one of the best forwards we ever had in Springfield. What for? I dunno . . . some peccadillo . . . the boy went off to a dance after a game or something. Trouble is, Don hasn't had any coaching experience with a real team. He's too young. I said that from the start. Considering what he had, he's done all right, although, of course, Kennedy developed some of the boys; but the trouble is I see it is he lacks experience; he's apt to go off half-cocked."

"Why, Daddy!" Everyone turned to look at Mrs. Shaw. "Daddy, you said last month he was the best young coach in the State. Didn't you?"

This time he heard her. In fact he had no choice.

"Now . . . now . . . hold on. Wait a minute. What I said was . . ." He finished his drink and held out his glass. "What I said was, he's done O.K. for a youngster. So he has, done well. But he never was anything more than a stopgap to my way of thinking. Fact is, if that old fool Peedad Wilson hadn't talked us into it, I doubt if we would have picked the boy. As usual Peedad wanted to embarrass me if he could. Well . . . I've got my eye on this fella, Charley Anderson of Richmond. There's a man with his feet on the ground; knows what it's all about.

What Springfield needs is a coach who's mature, who really knows his business, who can develop a winning team."

"But, Dad, I thought the boys all liked him. Tom does. Tom thinks he's wonderful."

"The boys! The boys! The boys! What does Tom know about it? You don't seem to understand, Mary Marcia, this isn't a class in kindergarten. This is basketball."

"Yes, but, Frank," she persisted. Few people ever argue with J. Frank about anything, and fewest of all took him on in a dispute over basketball which he knew so well. The whole room became silent, listening. "If he's good enough to take the team into the Finals of the State . . ."

"Ha! That's just it. He hasn't got us there yet, has he? No, sir. Besides, bear in mind one thing; he caught that Burris team on an off day. Caught 'em on their bad day, the one bad day they've had all season. Why, they were flat-footed out there all afternoon, flat-footed."

J. Frank knew his basketball and they could see it. To the suggestion that Burris was not playing their game that afternoon the local sympathizers all agreed. Obvious to everyone; Springfield had no right to win. They won; therefore, something was wrong. Unquestionably, as J. Frank explained it, Burris was flat-footed that afternoon. Everyone in the big room saw this save Mary Marcia.

"And was this Henderson lucky that Tom stayed in! That he didn't commit that fifth personal foul. Was Don lucky!" Again everyone agreed. Without Tom Shaw the Springfield team was only half a team. Besides catching Burris flat-footed on an off day, the Wildcats were lucky, Don was lucky, extremely lucky to win.

J. Frank would willingly have continued his analysis of the game, but the hostess called from the dining room. "Dinner, folks. We must eat if we're going to be back in the Field House this evening. Tommy always likes to be there when the teams come up."

In the poolroom, opposite the courthouse, there were two telephones. One was in the front of the store on the cigar stand, where a small, baldish man stood. Another was in a booth back of the four pool tables. Mike's Pool Parlor and Billiard Emporium was usually crowded at 5:30 on a Saturday afternoon. Every table was occupied the day of the Semifinals, and a number of kibitzers sat in high chairs or leaned against the walls on both sides, watching. The telephone in the front of the store was silent; but the one in the booth at the rear rang continuously. It was answered by the little, red-eyed chap who had observed the game from that seat in the middle of the stands in the afternoon.

"Hullo. Yeah . . . talking. Nope, they couldn't quite make it. Well, they almost nipped 'em at the end. Yeah, I think I can. Three hundred on Springfield? You want three hundred on Springfield? What's that? Fort Wayne, one to two, by four points; Springfield, three to two, by five points. O.K., Jack. Call me about seven-thirty and I'll know. But I think I can fix you up."

He rang off and went toward the rear of the room where there was a small desk. Unlocking a lower drawer, he drew out a dingy ledger and jotted down some figures. Before he had finished and shut the book the phone was ringing. He slapped the book in the drawer, locked it, and came back to the booth.

"Hullo? Yes. Oh, hullo, Mr. Johnson. Uhuh, they did. Well, we was both wrong. I say we was both wrong. Brother . . . that ain't nothing to what it cost me! Cost me plenty. Yeah. I think I can grab off some Fort Wayne dough for you;

there's a lot of people from up there in town this evening. How much you want? How much? O.K. It's Fort Wayne, one to two, by four points; Springfield, three to two by five points. O.K. Call me about seven-thirty and I'll let you know."

•

Two hours later the boys were back in the locker room at the Field House, dressed and ready to go. One or two were passing the ball around when Don, in his shirtsleeves, called them together. Once more they grouped around the benches, watching while he stood before them, looking over the notes he had made during the afternoon. He ran one finger of his left hand inside the collar of his shirt, yanked his head up, and spoke.

"First of all, I wantcha loose out there this evening. Get loose. You can't have any fun if you're tied up. Relax, all of you. I wantcha to relax, everyone. I want you to have some fun this evening. Basketball has to be fun, *it has to be fun.*

"Now, they play what we would term a center block-out. When they turn to come inside—get this, Walt—hold your position. Hold your position! The whole keynote of this is position—

heads-up defense. They fake a lot, Chuck. Don't get worried; don't get flustered; don't let 'em bother you. They fake and then come right back at the hole you left. See?

"This boy Benson, this colored boy of theirs, he's fast, awful fast. Tom, you're faster'n him. He very seldom passes; oh, very seldom. He's a shooter. Ramsay does a fake alla time. Jim, you'll be on him. Talk to him . . . nothing disrespectful, nothing rough; but keep up the old chatter." He glanced nervously at his watch. Russ Brainerd, at his elbow, spoke quietly.

"Three minutes."

"O.K. Now one thing, let's get clear. No beefin'! No matter how wrong the decisions are, no beefin'! Tom, if the going gets tough, take a time-out. We gotta get our heads up; we gotta go on these boys quick, real quick. Start moving, start scoring right away. You guards come over and feed that ball loose to the sides."

Down the row the jaws moved in unison.

"Tom! You follow up, will ya, get under that basket and follow up. Fake that pass in there, John. When a man makes a mistake, boys, pat him on the back. Pat him on the back, you guys. We're all gonna make mistakes; look at me, I've made plenty this season. If you make mistakes, forget 'em. We can't help our mistakes, no one can. You're a better ballclub than they are. They're not any super ballclub, not by any means. Sure, they won the State last year. What of it? This is this year.

"O.K. Strike hard and strike fast. Run me a lead out there right at the start. Keep your chins up . . . and le's go!"

17

Back in Springfield Peedad turned on his radio. The crowd roar instantly swept over his small living room. Passing through on her way upstairs, his wife looked at him listening in the easy chair.

"You always said this basketball was a disease. There you are like everyone else in Springfield this evening!"

"I'm listening on account of Don. I'm anxious to see him come through tonight. It would mean a great deal to him, and he's a good boy."

The bland voice of Buck Hannon at the microphone in Muncie interrupted him. ". . . So, folks, the score . . . at the end of the first quarter . . . Springfield, 8; Fort Wayne, 2. Let me repeat. The Springfield Wildcats lead the Fort Wayne Tigers here at the Field House, 8 to 2. The winner, as you know, is to go into the Finals in Indianapolis one week from tonight. And, folks, this is the way it went. Springfield was hot and grabbed off an early lead right at the start. John Little caged a short one-hander in the first sixty seconds, and MacDonald hit a long one, and then Tom Shaw hit, and Walt smacked one through the draperies to make it 8 to 0 before Charley Smithson connected on Fort Wayne's seventeenth shot. Shaw is covering Benson beautifully. He hasn't scored yet; he has that Fort Wayne boy bottled up. At the end of the quarter, then, the score stands 8 to 2 for the Wildcats, and Coach Murray is throwing in subs . . . Biggs for Chambers . . . Steele for Ramsay . . . and . . . yes . . . there goes Gardiner for Benson. Springfield had that boy Benson covered like a tent this quarter. They were using a pressing defense, crowding them close, while Fort Wayne is using a zone defense, waiting for a break into the basket.

"All right. Here's the whistle. A jump ball between Shaw and Steele. Little takes the tip . . . to Mac . . . over to Turner . . . to Tom in the corner . . . who throws . . . hits . . . nope . . . it's no good . . . now Fort Wayne comes down past the ten-second line . . . hullo . . . there's a foul on Little . . . yes . . . there goes Cox throwing. It's good, and the score now is: Springfield Wildcats, 8; Fort Wayne Tigers, 3.

"The Wildcats bring it in . . . to Turner . . . a long pass down the floor to Little . . . he's covered . . . back to Mac . . . to Jim . . . he throws . . . it's . . . no good . . . Little has the rebound . . . he tips it up . . . it's . . . good . . . another goal and the score is 10 to 3 in favor of the Wildcats.

"Fort Wayne brings it in . . . down the east side . . . to Cox . . . to Biggs . . . to Steele . . . Steele shoots . . . and scores a high one from way out . . . 10 to 5 . . . and now Springfield takes it in . . . over to Mac . . . to John . . . to Chuck . . . to Jim Turner . . . the ball is passed down the floor to Tom . . . he goes in under the basket . . . it's no good . . . there's a foul on Tom Shaw . . . a free throw, I *believe*.

"Yep. They parade back to the east foul line. Gardiner throws . . . no good . . . it's the Wildcats outa bounds . . . Mac dribbles down the south side of the floor to Tom . . . a bounce pass to Jim . . . who passes to John . . . he turns . . . shoots . . . *it's good* . . . and the score is now, 12 to 5, 12 to 5 for the Springfield Wildcats, and the crowd is just . . . about . . . going mad . . . here at the Muncie Field House. . . .

"Fort Wayne brings the ball in . . . from Cox to Steele . . . to Biggs . . . Biggs loses it to Little . . . what a game that boy Little has been playing . . . John dribbles . . . now he loses it . . . nope, it's a jump ball between Little and Steele . . . Shaw has it . . . he grabs the ball . . . now it's outa bounds under the Fort Wayne basket. It'll be the Wildcats outa bounds . . . in to Shaw . . . a bounce pass to Little . . . who's fouled . . . he's fouled as he shoots . . . so, it is two free throws for Springfield."

"Yea! Wildcats. Yea! Wildcats! Yea! Wildcats." A crescendo of cheering broke into the mike.

"The first one . . . it's no good . . . and . . . *and* the second is good. . . . Little gets one of those two points, making the score 13 to 5 for the Springfield Wildcats. They . . . they're simply running away with it. Now the Tigers have the ball . . . to Steele . . . to Biggs . . . and there's the whistle for the end of the half. With the score 13 to 5 for the Wildcats, 13 to 5 for the Kats . . ."

•

Down in the dressing room, Don yanked off his coat and rolled up his sleeves with those same nervous gestures. The five boys sat panting on the benches, towels over their necks, heads down. They had been tired between the halves of the afternoon game. Now they were almost all in, and he noticed this immediately. So he let them rest longer than usual and made his talk shorter.

"We set the tempo. Just like I asked you. That's good, that's perfectly all right. But don't you relax one second on defense. Tom, you did a first-class job on Benson, you sure did. They yanked him to rest him for this last half, and he'll make plenty of trouble, so watch him every minute. Naturally, they'd like for us to get listless on defense now, so they can start passing on us. Don't do it; don't do it.

"No, sir. Let's us do the passing. We're a passing ballclub, not a dribbling ballclub. Understand? Get me, Tom? See, Walt? Watch your fouls, John, watch 'em. They got three on you now, and the officials are awful darned sharp here. And keep your eyes *on the ball*."

•

Back in Springfield Peedad switched on a news broadcast between the halves and then turned the radio off.

"Who's winning?" asked his wife from the kitchen.

"Springfield. Way ahead at the half; 13 to 5. If he wins tonight, Don Henderson can be mayor of this town. Say, mebbe that isn't such a bad idea at that!" He sat down at the old-fashioned desk, which didn't seem in the least out of place in the room, and took up some papers. They kept his attention so long that it was some few minutes before he rose and switched on the radio to Buck Hannon and the Muncie Field House again.

". . . And at the end of the third quarter . . . Springfield Wildcats, 26; Fort Wayne Tigers, 19. The Wildcats started to chuck some long ones; they missed quite a few, and Johnny Benson came in there fast to grab that ball and help the Tigers make up some of that lead. In the first quarter they covered Benson like a shirt, but in this third quarter the colored boy broke loose, scored four field goals, and . . . well . . . here they go . . . a jump ball between Shaw and Benson."

"Yea! Wildcats. Yea! Wildcats! Yea! Wildcats."

"The ball is tipped in to Little . . . to Mac . . . he shoots from way out . . . it's no good . . . Shaw has the rebound off the bankboard . . . no good . . . Benson has it now . . . he fakes . . . a long pass to Chambers under the basket . . . he hits . . . and it's 26 to 21, and say . . . is this a ballgame?"

The yells from both sides swamped Peedad's little living room, even drowned out Buck's voice from time to time.

Out on the floor of the Field House, Don sat with the frown deepening over his eyes as the score mounted. Can we hold that lead; can we? They may do us an awful lot of harm yet; they sure stepped up on us fast. That's because our boys are tired. Tom's all in out there right now.

He watched the big chap dodge, feint, pass the ball, receive it back again, turn to go in, and stop, so closely guarded he couldn't move. Suddenly he broke loose and darted inside where he was met head-on by a Fort Wayne player, and the unintentional collision knocked them both to the floor. Don rose anxiously to his feet, watching while the team went to Tom's aid. John and Walt yanked him up, and he stumbled a few steps, one hand on his head.

Holy smoke, thought Don, if Tom's through we're finished! He's keeping them together; he's holding them in the game. The big boy staggered a minute, rubbed the back of his neck, straightened up, and then gave a quick glance toward the bench. His glance reassured Don, who sank back with relief. Behind him, the Springfield stands roared.

"Yea! Wildcats! Shaw . . . Shaw . . . Shaw . . . fight-team-fight!"

That boy has guts; he really has what it takes. And folks thought he was in there because he's a rich man's son, because he lived on the West Side, because I wanted to nail down my job. Well, they'll take all that back tonight.

The whistle blew. Out on the floor, for the hundredth time that day, Tom gathered himself to jump. His head throbbed painfully, his legs were numb, every muscle ached from his fall; only in the heat of conflict could he forget his exhaustion. He wiped his hands on his wet shirt front.

The referee held the ball, the whistle at his lips. Tom threw himself up, that long, black arm reaching with his. The ball fell away and was grabbed by Ramsay of Fort Wayne, who raced down the floor.

"Watch out there . . . John . . . cover up, Jim . . . watch him . . . cover!"

The Tigers passed it round the circle, back and forth, back and forth, waiting for a chance to get in, to break through the Wildcat defense. Suddenly one player fumbled momentarily and John was on the ball instantly. He made a fast break and was off. Once again that rush, once more that agonizing struggle under the basket, that terrific effort to work free; again those annoying arms waving in his face as he tried to pass. And all the time in his ears the quick, sharp cries of his teammates. He had the ball, he bounced it under Benson's arms to John, who faked, went in, and hooked it upward.

The ball rolled on the rim, fell away, and with despair in his heart, Tom saw Benson reaching up off the board and snatching it from John's outstretched fingers. Shoot! I shoulda been in there. I should have gone in and grabbed that ball.

Now Benson was weaving down, the whole field at his heels or panting by his side. He was covered, he passed, took it back, suddenly turned and shot from way out. He hit, and the score was 27 to 25.

This is gonna be a ballgame, and right here is the spot for our last time out.

Tom gathered them around: tired, panting, mouths open, sweat running down necks and faces. "Hey, Kats, c'mon now! Whassa matter, you dying on your feet? C'mon, only a few minutes to go. We must hold this lead. Are you gonna let Don down . . . after we had it all sewn up . . . are you gonna let him down . . . are you? Hey there, Chuck, hey, Walt . . . hey, Jim!"

They surged out, got the ball on the tip-off. But it was Tom who took it back from Chuck, who passed to Jim; Tom who cut over and received the pass back, and Tom who roared in to hit with a shovel pass and make it 29 to 25. For just a second he forgot his agony as he glanced at the clock. Two minutes, less than two to go. "C'mon, you guys, give it the works; give it everything you got."

Then Benson was free once more. The annoying, persistant, elusive Benson. Sneaking down the side, dribbling in, weaving through their defense, and throwing as usual from way out. He hit just above the basket, and missed. Summoning his final bit of energy, Tom jumped for it, but the colored boy was the fresher of the two and beat him by inches. Grabbing if off the board, he came down, made a quick shovel pass to a teammate at one side, who threw . . . and hit!

29 to 27.

Two points. Only two points and a minute and a half to go. Hug that ball, you guys, hug it . . . hullo . . . what's that . . . a foul on John . . . shucks . . . is that right . . . yes . . . his fourth . . . no, his fifth . . . hang it all, there goes John! Now we're really up against it with John out when we need him most. John was half the team. Those officials don't want us to win nohow.

"Shucks, John, that's tough luck; you didn't hook him, boy, I was watching alla time . . . shucks . . . you really played ball tonight, kid . . . you really did." He put his arm round the other's wet shoulder, as Cox of Fort Wayne rushed past and struck out a moist paw.

"Nice work, Little, nice work. Too bad you're through." The disconsolate boy said nothing, walking off the floor with his head down, as Joe Fisher, his sub, raced out. Over the din Tom heard Buck Hannon's voice shrieking behind him.

". . . Yes, here comes Joe Fisher, and two . . . three fresh subs for the Tigers. Biggs for Chambers, McConnell for Smithson . . . and Harrison for Cox. The score is: Springfield Wildcats, 29; Fort Wayne Tigers, 27. The Tigers are really climbing on the Kats' heels now. Less than two minutes of this grand ballgame left, and the whole crowd on their feet yelling."

They lined up beside the free throw lane. Tom focused his eyes on the basket. The ball swished past him in the air and fell cleanly through the bucket. They were leading by a single point.

Only one point ahead! It hung in the back of his brain, but there was no time to think, no time for anything save the fight, the fight to hold them, to contain them, to struggle against those newer, fresher men. No more chances, no more long shots, just hold it . . . hold it . . . hold it . . . from Walt to Jim . . . to Joe . . . now he had it . . . he turned quickly, slipped, and Benson cut across, nipping the ball out of his grasp.

He roared down, ducking, twisting, Tom desperate at his side, following every move, close to him every second, arms out, bottling him securely so he could not pass. There was a sudden snap under his arms to a teammate, then back it came, and Benson, pivoting suddenly, threw.

By the roar from the Springfield stands, Tom knew he had missed. A Fort Wayne player took it off the board, and Tom's heart leaped as he watched Walt lean over, grasp the ball, and create a jump-ball situation. Springfield regained possession. Now, then. Now you Kats, c'mon!

Down they went, slowly, cautiously, to Mac, to Tom, to Jim . . . hold it . . . Walt, squeeze that ball . . . to Mac again.

Again that form burst past him. Benson, nipping in with catlike quickness, intercepted the ball and swung toward the Fort Wayne goal. Tom raced along at his side, when suddenly he heard the referee's whistle. He glanced up. A foul on Benson for charging his defensive man. The teams stopped, hesitated, reversed their field and went toward the Fort Wayne goal, as Benson slapped the ball to the floor with disgust. Time was slipping away.

Someone threw it to Tom. They moved to the

free throw zone. So easy when you're fifty feet away in the stands; so easy when you're on the bench, waiting to go. Easy, too, when you are practicing in your own gym with no one to watch. But here, out here, alone before six thousand shrieking maniacs, everyone on his feet yelling, it isn't so easy. Everyone was watching him, most of all his own crowd; Jim, blinking behind those misty glasses, and Walt, with the sweat pouring off his slender neck, and Chuck, with his mouth open and the fatigue showing in the lines on his face, and Joe Fisher, nervous, tight, anxiety betrayed by the way he held him in his glance. All looking to him. It's easy in practice. It isn't easy when you are out there alone, leading by a single point, with the game in its dying seconds and those Tigers crawling closer, closer, closer.

Now then. Steady. Relax. Don always said to relax, to take it easy. Basketball's gotta be fun, it's gotta be fun. Bounce the ball a couple of times. Fingers loose. Watch it now. This will sew things up; this will do the trick.

The ball hit the rim of the basket, rolled round and round, and at last fell through just as he raced in and grabbed it with the last ounce of effort left. He came down hugging the ball, Benson hugging it also.

Right there the gun sounded.

•

Inside Peedad's living room Buck Hannon's tones became a shriek. "THERE'S THE END OF THE GAME. THE END OF THE GAME. The score, 30 to 28, in favor of the Springfield Wildcats. Tubby, hey there, Tubby, get some of the boys over here. Folks, we're trying now to get some of the Wildcats to come to the mike . . . the crowd's really going wild now . . . they're tearing away at the baskets . . . two of the Kats are up there cutting 'em down . . . Jim! Jim, c'mon over here. Howsit feel, Jim? Tell the radio audience how it feels to be in the Finals!"

A hoarse, jerky voice screamed into the mike, "It really feels swell." Then Buck Hannon intervened.

"Thank *you*, Jim Turner. And here comes Tom Shaw who played such a magnificent game under those bankboards all day. He's the boy who stood off Benson of Fort Wayne Central so he was bottled up most of the game. Tom, howsit feel, boy?"

"*Yeaaa . . .*"

"And, folks, here's John Little who did such a grand job out there. John has a piece of the net round his neck."

"Yowser. We're really in there now."

"You bet you are, John. And, folks, I'd like to get Bob Murray, the coach of the Tigers, and Don Henderson, but Murray has left the floor and so have the rest of the Fort Wayne boys . . . but they've got nothing to be ashamed of, nothing. They played a grand game . . . and don't let anybody tell you different. Here comes Don Henderson wiping the perspiration off. Ha-ha, Don, tell us how you feel now."

"Oh, boy! It's a swell feeling, Buck. But Fort Wayne has a grand ballclub; they're a fine team, only they had some tough luck out there at the start."

"They sure did . . . well, folks, that was Don Henderson, the coach of this gallant Springfield team that has fought its way against odds into the Finals. No one thought they'd come through except Don . . . Is that right, Don?"

"Buck, I knew the kids would come through if I asked the impossible of 'em."

"That's fine, Don, that's fine . . . and thank you . . . and congratulations to your splendid team. Well, folks, that about brings our broadcast to a close, all except the statistics by Dick Lewis, the sports editor of the *Springfield Tribune*. Dick is waiting to give them to you. C'mon in, Dick, and have a seat."

"Thanks, lots, Buck, but if you don't mind I'll stand, because seven thousand five hundred people are standing and I'd look kinda foolish sitting down in the middle of this madness. Folks, you people back home in Springfield have no idea how this place has gone wild. Everyone on their feet yelling for our Wildcats, and little boys and big boys and men who are grown-up boys all jumping for a piece of those tattered nets."

"Excuse me a second, Dick. Just let me interrupt a minute, please. Here's Mayor Swanson of Muncie, to say a word. C'mon in, Mayor Swanson."

A deep, powerful voice, one quite evidently used to speaking to crowds, boomed out.

"Congratulations, Springfield! You've got a grand team! I'm pulling for you to win the State, and I believe you've got the best team. Good luck!"

"Thanks, Mayor Swanson. Now, Dick, go on with those statistics, will you, please?"

"O.K., Buck. Turner had four buckets, two

free throws, and two personal fouls. John Little, who shot 'em high and shot 'em from every angle all day, had four baskets, three throws, and . . ."

•

Surrounded by the squad, Don was swept downstairs. The quiet, empty room which they had left was packed. A mob of strangers stood waiting. Some he knew; a reporter or two, a number of Springfield businessmen with whom he was slightly acquainted, and several friendly coaches. But the majority he had never seen before. He wondered how they got there. And were still getting there, for more strangers continued to sweep down the stairs, thrusting aside the protesting guard at the door above.

Springfield had arrived. So, too, had Don Henderson. Now they were news in Indiana.

18

Don was standing in the coach's room in the gym, talking with Dick Lewis and an Associated Press sportswriter who was making the rounds of the four towns whose teams were to compete in the Finals at Indianapolis that Saturday. In the two days since the Muncie Semifinals, Don had met many sportswriters he had never before seen. Many of them had suddenly discovered Springfield and the Wildcats. Obviously, they all agreed, Anderson was the favorite. On the early season record, Anderson ought to win. They had humbled Springfield once quite easily and were due to repeat. Yet the Wildcats were one of the four contending teams, so most reporters dropped off to spend a casual afternoon and pick up a column for the next day's paper. Dick Lewis, who knew everyone, introduced them around.

As usual that afternoon Don held a basketball in his hands. While he talked, he bounced it against the floor. Occasionally he tossed it into the air, hit it with his fist upwards, and caught it once more.

From across the hall came the shouts and songs of the boys, dressing.

"Hoo-ray for Jim . . . hoo-ray for Jim . . . hoo-ray for Jim . . . he's a darn nice guy."

The visiting fireman asked a question. "Well, how much of a lead *would* you consider safe in the last quarter, Don?"

Don, who didn't even remember the man's last name, thought a minute. "At the start of the last quarter? I wouldn't feel safe unless we were 12 points ahead. Maybe in the Finals not even that; maybe more."

"Look what happened over at La Porte on

Saturday!" suggested Dick. "Anything can happen in basketball."

"Anything can," agreed the other reporter. "How they feel after Muncie? Still loose?"

"Listen to 'em," said Don. The three men listened to the yelling across the hall. "We ought to be right mentally on Saturday. Yes, sir! They were loose yesterday at practice, I can tell you. They're rarin' up for this ballgame, and when these boys are up for a game, they're tough."

"Even against Anderson? Too bad you drew Anderson in the first game. You've got the tough side of that draw."

"Shoot! I'd rather play the tough team first. I'm weak in replacements. I'd much rather tackle Anderson in the afternoon when we're fresh. We've got nothing to lose, have we? They beat us by ten points or more in January. O.K., but three of my men were sick. Chuck didn't play, neither did Jim Turner or Walt MacDonald."

"No, but that boy Jackson Piper was in there then."

"That's correct. But John Little is just as good today. Tell you what; this gang is a different aggregation from the five that played early this year, and don't you forget it. They're really a ballclub now."

"Think it will give 'em the buck to play in the Coliseum?"

"Why should it? Oh . . . they might be a bit uneasy at the start, same as they were against Burris last Saturday afternoon at Muncie. It won't last long. These kids have their feet on the ground. They've come up the hard way, from defeat and disaster; they know their strength now."

Right at that moment Russ Brainerd entered. "Hullo there, Dick . . . hullo." He shook hands with the stranger. "Don, he wants to see you over at the office."

Don, who had begun to get ready for practice, put on his coat. "S'cuse me." He went out and up the stairs into the school itself and along the straight corridors with classrooms on both sides. In the Principal's outer office was a crowd of boys and girls, waiting excitedly for tickets at the counter. He opened the inner door to the Principal's room and went inside. Mr. Hinton was seated at a desk with piles of tickets and piles of dollar bills heaped upon it.

"Tickets . . . tickets . . . tickets. I'm nothing but a ticket seller these days—this week," said the Principal. He blinked behind his glasses, which accentuated the worried look on his face. "I haven't done a thing all week but look after these tickets. Believe me, if I had thirty thousand I could get rid of every one. It's got so now I just don't answer the phone except on long-distance calls. And there's plenty of them, too!"

"I know. You aren't telling me anything. They're all on my neck the same way."

"Sit down, Don." The elder man leaned toward him. "Don, I wanted real bad to have a chance for a word or two. This is the first opportunity I've had to congratulate you and tell you what a wonderful job you've done at Springfield. The school is proud of you." He took off his glasses, wiped them, held them up to the light and snapped them on again.

"Grand spirit, too. The boys have done better'n could be expected. But I wonder . . . Don . . . you're a fine coach and a fine feller, but I'm a wee bit . . . afraid . . . you aren't always as tactful as you might be."

I don't guess maybe I am. But what on earth is he after? What's biting him, anyway?

"Hope you'll let me say these things because I'm older'n you, and I've been here in Springfield quite some time. D'you . . . maybe . . . you tend to act and speak before you think sometimes."

This only confused Don more. His face showed his amazement. What in the world is he getting at? Why doesn't he come out from behind his beard?

"What I mean to say is, some of our good citizens here in town feel you're a little mite . . . a little bit standoffish . . . just a little . . . yes?"

"Who? How? What . . . who says so?"

"Don, these things get around. Understand me now. I'm not criticizing you; don't want you to think for a minute I'm criticizing. I'm only saying these things for your own good. We want you to stay here real bad. I'll do whatever I can myself for you. Only I think I should warn you that you have made some enemies in Springfield."

Enemies! Russ Brainerd said the same thing. Others had said it. This time Don didn't laugh as he had several months previously. The enemies hadn't mattered then, just as they hadn't mattered at Center Township, because he wasn't up in front. Now he was the coach of a winning team and on the spot. He began to understand.

The elder man continued. "Of course, Don, I'm no coach myself and don't pretend to know anything about the game; but it was apparent even to me last Saturday night over at Muncie that you were mighty short of substitutes. Now, if—if maybe you hadn't been quite so hasty and refused to let Tim Baker come back on the team . . ."

"I hadn't any choice, Mr. Hinton."

"Yes, mind you, I'm not saying you weren't right. I'm just saying if you hadn't been quite so hasty about it, well, he'd be mighty useful over at Indianapolis this weekend. Wouldn't he? Not, of course, that it makes any difference, but you have to be careful how you go about things in Springfield. A man can do a lot if he has tact, if he goes about things tactfully."

"Exactly what do you mean, Mr. Hinton? I don't believe I get you."

"Well, perhaps you didn't know, but Tim's father is the president of the Chamber of Commerce and a powerful man downtown. He'd set his heart on the boy playing and winning the Trester Award. And it really hurt him the worst way when the kid got thrown off the team. Now you don't go for to hurt anybody, do you, Don?

There's a way of doing everything, and I'm afraid you weren't tactful when you acted like that— without thinking things through."

Don tried to speak. He had lots he wanted to say. A dozen sentences bubbled up and struggled to come out. He stuttered and stammered and ended by saying nothing. So the elder man went on.

"What I'm about to say now perhaps I really shouldn't. But I like you and I mean it when I tell you that; so does everyone around here, and we all want you to come back. There's a rumor, just a rumor, you understand, that the School Board isn't too anxious to renew your contract next season. I'm just tipping you off on this."

Don closed the door, walked past the gang of kids clamoring for seats in the outer office, and down the long hall. So J. Frank is after me. O.K. I'll fool him. I'll win the State! Then the Governor himself couldn't appoint anyone else to coach the Wildcats.

He returned to his little room and changed into his practice clothes: the sweat shirt, the old pants, the basketball shoes. He slung his whistle around his neck. Across the hall the boys were still dressing in a cheerful din. He heard Dick

Lewis, standing at their door, shout, "You boys get through Anderson first. Anderson's the team to beat. You'll win the State if you get past Anderson."

Tom Shaw's high-pitched voice echoed across to him. "We'll win the State. Period."

19

Old-timers could recall when the town of Springfield really went mad over basketball. They'll tell you about Elmer Sternberger's team, the Wildcats of 1938, who won their way into the Finals, and how folks stormed the gym to get seats. That year tickets were due to go on sale at four of a March afternoon. By six o'clock that evening before, a lone customer had appeared at the front entrance to the Hanson Gymnasium. It was cold, so he stood kicking his feet and stomping them on the pavement to keep warm. By eleven there were six hundred foot-stompers in line. A few had brought radios, kerosene heaters, and some sat on stools around bonfires, playing cards. Enterprising youngsters did a good business all night rushing hot dogs and coffee from Joe's Lunch on West Mulberry. At two in the morning the line of a thousand persons extended as far as Buckeye and Superior Streets. At three the snow began. At four the crowd was so large the police were called out, and at five someone routed the school authorities from their beds. The tickets went on sale at six. Within one hour they were all sold. Hundreds of disgruntled citizens went home to bed.

In those days Springfield really supported the Wildcats. Today, the old-timers said, the town is soft. Nowadays tickets are drawn by lot in an atmosphere of comparative sanity and decorum in the gymnasium. Things aren't what they used to be!

That evening a thousand or more season ticket holders, the only citizens whose applications for seats at Indianapolis were even considered, sat along one side of the bleachers in the warm gym. In the middle of the floor was a table with a steel wastepaper basket upon it. The Principal stepped forward. He looked around a minute at the restless crowd before speaking. They became quiet when he began to talk.

"I have here . . ." He waved the cards in his hand . . . "I have here the applications you folks made this week for tickets to the Finals at Indianapolis on Saturday. Now, as you all must know, there aren't enough tickets to go round. We'll give them out just as long as they last, and we assume you realize you may be disappointed; that you understand the rules of the game and will participate in them. Every season ticket holder has a chance for as many tickets as he has season tickets. That is, if you had two season tickets, you'll be permitted if your name is called to buy two tickets for the Finals. I shall put the applications here in this container, and ask Pearl to come up and draw them out."

A buzz went over the stands. It was a warm, friendly, and neighborly crowd: lots of businessmen, farmers in boots and overshoes, students who had received no seats in the school allotment and hoped to go to Indianapolis with their parents. The stands joked and laughed and called to each other, for everyone knew everyone else. In the middle of the front row were J. Frank Shaw and Mary Marcia.

As the Principal spoke again, the chatter and noise stopped. "Has anyone a question to ask?" Apparently nobody had any question. They knew their chance for a seat was slight; but there was always a chance and many fans had turned out to see the fun. "All right then; if your name is called, step right over there to that table under the balcony. Please stay off the basketball floor. Go over to that table, pay your two-twenty, and get your seat. Is that clear?" He looked round anxiously. "O.K., then; good luck to all of you."

He dumped the batch of application cards into the steel wastepaper basket and shook them up. The girl at his side stepped forward and put her hand within. She pulled out a card, looked at it, smiled, and gave it to him. The Principal glanced at the name and smiled, also.

"Mr. and Mrs. Kenneth Humphries." A sudden roar swept the room, followed by a burst of applause as a man picked his way carefully down the bleachers through the crowd and went over toward the table under the balcony. Everyone knew the Humphries. They had been Wildcat fans and attended every game for twenty years.

"Mr. and Mrs. Roscoe Smith." No response. He waited. "Not here? All right; we'll hold them then." Another slip was handed to him. "Ward R. Eagle."

Again the roar, sudden and spontaneous, as a man worked his way down the stands. He was a popular worker in the post office, known to everyone in town.

"Mr. and Mrs. Cecil Little." A thunder of cheers greeted John Little's dad as he stepped down from the top row of the bleachers. "Mr. Walter Kemp." He, also, was well received. Every citizen in town knew that Mr. Kemp had long made a practice of taking a dozen kids to the basketball games. "Raymond and Martha Maddox."

The line was growing under the balcony. The Principal read from another card. "Deke Noble."

"Wow! Wowser!"

"Deke! Hey, Deke! Hey there!"

A bald-headed man stepped from his seat amid yells and cheers. The town knew that Deke, the managing editor of the *Tribune*, would be unable to leave town that Saturday afternoon. "Hey, Deke! Lemme buy it off you." "Deke! Wanna sell your seat, Deke?"

"Mead Trowbridge." "Jack C. Dawson." Names came faster; the line at the table beneath the balcony now stretched across the whole end of the floor. Don, standing by the entrance to the dressing rooms downstairs, noticed J. Frank, his hat and ulster on his lap, twisting nervously as time passed, as the available supply of tickets diminished and his name was still uncalled. Maybe, he thought, this is a good time to get away. So he slipped down, got his hat and coat, and walked out the side entrance to the gym. As he came round front, excited and delighted ticket-holders were coming down the main steps, calling to each other in cheery tones. A heavy snow was falling, and he was sludging along when he heard his name.

"Don! Wait a minute."

"Why, Mrs. Shaw!" She was bundled up in a luxurious leopardskin coat, the only one of its kind in town.

"Are you going now? Frank's sticking it out to the end but I'm leaving. This storm is terrible. Can I take you home in my car?"

"Thanks, that would be just fine if you'd drop me off at my place, Mrs. Shaw. Snow is sure thick tonight, isn't it?"

"The car's over here." They walked along the street to where her Chrysler was parked and got in. She backed a little and then swing deftly away from the curb.

"This ticket business is something, isn't it?" Immediately he wished she had chosen another subject.

"Yes, it is."

"I guess you haven't had a very pleasant time this week, Don?"

"I'll say! They've been on my neck every minute—long-distance calls from Greencastle and Lafayette and even Gary for tickets. Sunday it got so I didn't try to answer the phone. Finally, one feller insisted he should talk to me; he said he *had* to talk to me. Seems he was a farmer out at Center Township, man by the name of Earl Whitely; I used to board with him my first year there. Know what? Earl offered to kill a hog for me if I'd get him a couple of seats."

"Is that right?"

"Yes, and then Sunday evening I was over to the Emerson's for supper, and a man came and asked for me. Mrs. Shaw, I don't know to this day how he figured I was there, but he did. When I went to the door, he handed me a big bundle;

didn't want anything and wouldn't even tell me his name. Just gave me a great big ham, all cooked and ready to eat!"

"My goodness! A ham! Is that so? What did you say?"

"I thanked him. I said, 'Brother, that's fine and all that and I'm sure grateful, but how you gonna feel if we lose that first game on Saturday afternoon?' "

"What did he say to that?"

"Oh, he was dead certain he'd feel just exactly the same. That it wouldn't make a mite of difference."

"But you won't lose the first game, will you? That's against Anderson, isn't it?"

"Mrs. Shaw, I don't aim to lose any of them. But you never can tell. However, I'll say this: Anderson is the team to beat over there."

"You'll win. I know you will. Tom says so." But her mind was still on the ticket situation. "I must say, I shouldn't think the Emersons would have trouble getting tickets." Her voice was stiff. "They have two girls in High School, and one got through last year."

"No, ma'am, being in High School doesn't get you anything. The kids have to draw same as the older folks. Mr. Hinton told me the other day there just aren't enough seats to go round. He said he could sell thirty thousand tickets in this town, and I believe he could. There was an editorial in the *Press* the other night giving the exact number allotted to kids and to adults. That's the first time I've seen the figures in print."

"Oh! That horrid Peedad! Did you see what he said about Frank and the municipal sewerage system? And then that editorial about this town being basketball crazy and basketball being a disease and all that."

"You wouldn't deny this town is basketball crazy, would you?"

"Yes, but he said the tickets or most of them went to over-stuffed businessmen and not to the school."

"Hold on. He didn't mean J. Frank. J. Frank has the same figure he had when he played center for Butler. Besides, the chap's right, I think."

"I'm afraid you don't understand, Don. For most folks a couple of tickets to the Finals would be fine. But Dad's the Republican Committee-man from this State, and he has so many friends he has to take care of."

"Why?"

"Don't you see? He has to. They're after him from all over the State, from all over the Mississippi Valley."

"Mrs. Shaw, lemme ask you a question. Who's playing at Indianapolis on Saturday?"

"Why, Anderson . . . and La Porte . . . and Evansville and Springfield."

"Sure. But who is Springfield? Mr. Benson, the president of the Merchants National, or Mr. Rogers or Mr. Baker, the head of the Chamber of Commerce? Not for me, it isn't. Red Crosby and Dorothy Allen, that's who Springfield is down there at Indianapolis. It's the kids, not the rest of us older folks. That's who seats should go to; it's their team. Not ours."

She sniffed again. "I can imagine what the Coliseum would be like Saturday if it was filled with fifteen thousand High School brats. Why, it would be a madhouse!"

"Judging by what happened to us over at Marion a couple of weeks ago, my guess is they'd behave as well as the grown folks, as the businessmen in town."

The snow swirled against the windshield. They reached his house. She stopped the car and snapped off the ignition. The wiper ceased clicking. "Well, let's not worry about that. I want to ask you a favor. Not for myself, though. Not for Dad, either."

"I'd do anything I could for Tom's family." Anything except seats for the Finals, that is. He braced his feet against the floorboards.

"It isn't for me, it's for you. Don, there are folks in town who don't like you. When you threw those boys off the squad last year you built up quite considerable resentment; you must have realized that. Now these people and their friends would like to get a new coach next year, if they could."

"That's not exactly news, Mrs. Shaw."

"No, probably not. But Dad does like you so much. He was a bit disappointed you didn't accept his offer to help out with Jerry Kates."

"Mrs. Shaw, the boys voted against it."

"In a way that hurt him worst of all. He and Tom had a terrible argument about it, and they don't see eye to eye on it all. He feels you could have won them over if you'd wanted to."

"I let the boys vote; they voted against it; that's all there was to the proposition."

"Anyhow, he was disappointed; and then he was also a little hurt you didn't help with those tickets over at Muncie. Y'know, he had to buy them from speculators at the last minute. Now. . ." Here it comes, here it comes, I thought so. "Now I realize you can't go handing out seats to every Tom, Dick, and Harry; but most probably if you went to Mr. Hinton he could get his hands on a couple. Couldn't he manage to dig up two seats?"

"Most probably he could."

"Only two, Don; a sort of gesture, understand? Dad would be so pleased it would make him forget that whole Kates affair. He's reasonable, he understands your position, he knows the pressure you're under, for he's been through it himself. But if you could . . ."

"Save my job by handing Mr. Shaw two seats for the Finals this week?"

With a gesture she pulled the leopard coat around her shoulders and tightened it at the neck. "Don't be that way. Please see his view-point. I'm thinking of you; I know what you've done for Tom and how he loves you. He does, you know, he really loves you. He's never been like this about any teacher or any coach before, and he wants you to stay in this town. So does Frank. We need young men like you; Springfield needs them badly."

His feet were braced. No, not one, not a single ticket.

"Mrs. Shaw, I'd like to put it up to you. Should I break a rule I've had all my coaching career for J. Frank? Should I?"

"Don, would you break it for Tom? If Tom asked you?"

That was harder. He stiffened in his seat; that made it harder. If Tom asked . . . why not? What's the difference? Fellow might as well be tactful, and everyone said he had no tact. He could hand the seats to Tom, and let Tom give them to his dad. What Tom did with them was his business. Springfield became more desirable than ever; the town, the familiar streets, the whole place, his work, and the boys. Especially the boys, his boys, who had come up together with him, the kids who had taken the lickings as juniors and sophs, and now as seniors were a winning team.

After all, why not?

Then his training intervened. The years of struggle on the court and off, the refusal to give in, came to the surface. He was conditioned to fight for what he felt, for what was closest to him. Two tickets or twenty, it was all the same.

If a man has to buy his job that way, he'd better not fool himself. Better say no and have it over with.

The forefinger of his left hand tugged nervously inside the collar of his shirt.

"Mrs. Shaw, I could get J. Frank those seats. But look, if I broke the rule for him I'd have to do it for others. For old friends of mine and my dad's, too; folks I've known all my life; Mr. Stevenson, the banker at home who gave me enough money to go through college. I've refused these people and I have to refuse you. I want to stay in Springfield. But if I can't, O.K. I can always go back to Center Township or some small school. In a way I was happier there. The kids are fine here, but, well . . . I guess it's the grown folks . . . no matter what you say about Peedad Wilson, he really had something in that editorial on basketball."

"Oh . . . that horrid man . . . that . . ."

"Hold on! He's right about this. When a town like Springfield gets seven hundred tickets and only two hundred and fifty or three hundred go to the kids, something is wrong. The team belongs to the kids. You believe that, don't you? You believe it's Tom's team, not ours."

"Yes, I believe that. Only this is the way things are run in Springfield, and I don't guess you'll ever change them. I shan't ask again."

Her words were a reproach. "I'm sorry, I'd like to. You understand, don't you?"

She switched the ignition key in the lock. The click of the key and the sound of the windshield wiper startled him. He got out.

"Good night, Mrs. Shaw. Thanks for the ride."

"Good night, Don." The door slammed. The car moved away. He stood watching the snow slur out from under the wheels.

20

"J ust one more, please, Mr. Henderson. Just one more." Photographers are never satisfied. "See here, you fellas, we have work to do this afternoon."

"O.K., boss. Just one more. Now lean over a little, boys, right hand on the right knee. Like that. There! That's fine." The team wore their white practice uniforms, with blue edging around the shoulders and blue belts. Don was in the center in his white sweatshirt. He hardly looked older or different from the others. "Hold it . . . there!" Flashbulbs exploded in the lighted gymnasium.

"Finished? This is our last practice and we have lots of work to do."

"Hold everything!" shouted another cameraman. There were half a dozen photographers taking their pictures that afternoon, for the press of the United States had suddenly discovered the Springfield Wildcats. "Now go in there one by one and shoot a few baskets, will ya kindly?"

The cameraman lined up the basket with his machine, pacing off the distance with considerable care. He held his flashbulb in his left hand. Each boy went in with the ball under the basket, and each was snapped in the act of shooting the ball into the hoop. Don stood at one side, watching nervously, glancing from time to time at his wristwatch. It was getting late. At last, everyone was satisfied; the camermen, picking up their tripods and equipment, left the floor, and the serious work of the afternoon began.

"All right now, le's go. Loosen up a little. Shoot a few first, for about five-six minutes, just get yourselves warmed up." For the last time before the Finals the gym echoed to the pound-

pound-pound of feet, the gentler thud-thud of balls, and the heavy breathing of the players. In practice sessions there were not two but six baskets hung up, one at each end and four more on extra bankboards suspended from each side of the balcony. They were all in use by the running, leaping Wildcats.

After a while Don gave two sharp toots on his whistle. The squad stopped and gathered round in a circle, wiping perspiration off their faces. He stood in the middle, bouncing the ball on the floor, and thinking, This is it, the last practice, the last practice of all.

"Now this Anderson team we meet over there on Saturday afternoon is the favorite. You all know that. If they're favorites, that's just fine with us. The newspapers have made 'em the winner; but I rather think you boys have proved this year that games aren't won in the sports columns. If they were, a lotta guys'd be out of work," he added savagely, tapping the ball end-lessly on the floor. "Now I b'lieve we oughta be right mentally to take these boys. It's quite true they beat us badly last January. We weren't a team then; moreover, Jim didn't play or Walt or Chuck. This time it'll be different. They're the favorites. O.K., that's all right. Let's us go over there and knock 'em off. I know we can.

"Remember, all of you, your mental attitude is important. No matter what happens, play your hardest; if you're way ahead, play harder. If you're behind, play harder; play your hardest all through the game, every single minute. Now, lemme see . . . oh, yes! Once in a while over there at Muncie this just naturally came up. Tom threw to Mac . . . over here . . ." He grabbed the boy by the arm and placed him, placed another. "Jim . . . you cut . . . hold it . . . there! Did we work on that? Nope? Well, when that situation comes up, when that man keeps going around, then Tom throws . . . overhand . . . right over his noggin. Flips it like this." He tossed the ball over Tom's tall figure. "Get the idea? Only once or twice in a ballgame, once or twice you might have that opportunity."

A brown, mongrel dog ambled up the staircase from below and romped out upon the floor. Russ Brainerd, standing behind the group, chased him toward the front door.

"This is our last chance to correct one or two of those faults that showed up at Muncie. We've got a lot of work to do, so let's go. Start with three on one side, three on the other; then we'll practice some outa bounds plays." Again the pound-pound-pound of feet, the softer thud-thud of balls on the floor. Time went by, the shadows lengthened outside, the boys became tired, but still he drove them. He was as weary as they were and once he betrayed the strain.

"Jim! Concentrate when you shoot. You weren't even looking that time; I was watching. Concentrate, every one of you; look when you shoot." Suddenly his voice became louder, with a harsh note in it. *"Hey there! You boys are asleep. Everyone wake up. That's better. Take that pivot, Tom, take that pivot. Speed . . . speed . . . more speed!"* He blew his whistle and they gathered around, panting and breathing heavily.

"See here, you all know our reputation. We depend on a fast break and high speed to get under that basket. Don't we? Huh? All right then, show me some speed, will ya?"

It was an hour later before practice was ended and forty minutes after that when Don, dressed, walked into the school building. As he passed down the corridor, a girl came out of one of the almost empty rooms, and he thought he heard sobs in the still hallway. He caught up with her and found her crying.

"Hey there, what's all this about? What seems

to be the matter?" He looked at her and saw it was Betty Jane Emerson, one of the seniors. "Why, Betty Jane! What's troubling you this evening?"

"I didn't get to go with the team." The sobs increased.

For a minute he was puzzled. "How's that?"

"I can't get to see the team play in the Finals."

"Hold on. Wait a minute. You mean you lost out on your ticket for Saturday?"

"Uhuh. And it's my team . . . mine . . . not theirs."

Don was uncomfortable. He understood perfectly what she meant. He also realized that, whatever happened, J. Frank and Denny Rogers' father and Mr. Benson would somehow find their way into the Coliseum on Saturday afternoon.

"See here! You come right along with me, Betty Jane. I intend to get you in there somehow." Wiping her eyes, the girl straightened up. They reached the office of the Principal, but the door was locked and everyone had left. Don was upset. He knew tickets for the Finals seldom remained unsold very long. The Principal, as he remembered, had advised him to ask early for whatever seats he wanted.

"Come on, let's us walk uptown a piece while I sorta think this over. Tell me what happened." They walked along Superior Street, the girl forgetting her distress. She felt the coach could help if anyone could. Don wanted to help, yet he wondered just how he could. Even for a coach, seats to the Finals were hard to obtain.

"You see," she explained, as if he didn't already know it, "seats are hard to get. Everyone in town is after them. There's two or three businessmen in town who buy up the kids."

"Buy up the kids?"

"Yes, men with money like Tom Shaw's dad. They get the kids to put in applications, and if they draw seats the older men buy them and give the kids a couple of dollars."

Holy smoke, thought Don, I'm the coach of the school and how little I really knew about what's going on. "Say! Does Tom know that?"

"He knows it takes place; he doesn't know his father is doing it. Lots of businessmen in town get their seats that way. Oh, well, maybe not lots. After all, when the faculty has been taken care of, that only leaves two hundred and thirty-five tickets from our allotment."

"How many kids want to go, do you imagine?"

"The Senior Council figures about eight hundred. A few might get to go with their parents."

"But the majority will stay home, is that it?"

She hesitated a second. "That's it. And we feel it's wrong."

Certainly something was wrong. Cautiously he tried to reassure her. "I think I may be able to get you one tomorrow." Although now that the Principal's office was closed for the day, he was far from hopeful.

"We think it's all wrong," she continued. "Now, for instance, the kids can get seats to any of the regular games during the season at school for a quarter. But if they happen to come to school the day of the game without any money, they have to show up in the evening at the gym and pay adult prices."

"How much is that?"

"Fifty cents. And lots of the kids can't afford it."

Once again he reflected, I'm the coach of the school; I'm close to them, much more so than any teacher. Yet how little I really know of what they think and feel.

The girl went on. "And it's our team . . . not theirs. Know what I think? I think basketball would be all right if it weren't for the older people."

"Funny you should say that. I've been thinking along the same lines myself lately." Only I never thought it clean through as you have. Kids are wonderful, aren't they? Peedad is correct; the kids are all right; it's the older folks who make trouble.

Say! There's an idea. I'll just go upstairs and ask Peedad what to do in a jam of this kind. I bet he'll have an idea for me. "Betty Jane, come in here to Walgreen's and have a coke. I'm going to get you a seat for the Finals on Saturday if it's the last thing I do."

And it may be just about that, in this town.

"Will you, honest? Will you? Oh, that would be wonderful."

They went to the counter and sat down. The place was nearly empty. "See here, you wait for me a few minutes, please. I want to go over this whole problem with someone I know upstairs."

Peedad's office was right next door. He went up the steps two at a time, despite his fatigue. As he expected, the little man was there, sitting at the roll-top desk in the dingy office. He was glad to see his visitor, and quickly removed some proofs and papers from a chair. Don told the story in a few words.

Peedad hoisted his feet up on the desk and took up a pipe as dingy and worn as the rest of the room. He laid his feet tenderly on a vast pile of letters, manuscripts, proofs, and other documents. "Well, Don, I figgered you was in for a spell of trouble. J. Frank hasn't been so voluble about you lately in Board meetings."

"You were dead right when you said that as soon as anyone crossed the Shaws they found themselves in trouble."

"Yeah, heh, heh. Well, I shouldn't worry if I was you, Don. You've produced a winning team, that's what they want. As long as you do that they won't fire you. Springfield wants a winner; the merchants like it 'cause it brings business to town; folks come in to see the team play, and it advertises us all over the State. The Frank Shaws want it because they're old players. When you don't win, they'll make you head scout or health education teacher or something of the sort."

"I won't wait for that; I'll resign."

"And we'll lose you. That's my objection to basketball. Folks in town get hysterical about it. They'll use anyone in order to win, including the kids. And the betting—it's heavy this year. Jim MacDonald was telling me yesterday a man called him on the phone the other evening and wanted to know how Walt's ankle was, whether he'd play Saturday."

"What for? What did Mac say?"

"'Cause he wanted to go heavy on the Kats to win. Mac was pretty sore; he just says, 'You better ask Coach Henderson.'"

"I wish he had."

"He wouldn't dare. That's why he called Mac. Three years ago we had a boy fired off the squad who left school and joined the Navy; kid felt he was disgraced. His parents didn't hear a word from him for seven weeks. And the year before you came, Tommy Casey was telling me, his boy and two other kids on the team were sick, didn't go to school or anything; but they showed up every day for basketball practice. Tom said the kid would burst into tears if he forbade him to go out. Why, the whole community's depending on 'em."

"I just heard something else I didn't know. Seems some of the businessmen got the kids to apply and then bought up their tickets at premium. Imagine, and Mrs. Shaw asking me for seats!"

The feet came down off the desk with considerable rapidity. Peedad sat up. Don saw where those peppery editorials came from. "You mean to say . . . to sit there and tell me Frank Shaw tried to bum tickets off you?"

"Sure, why not?"

"Why not! Besides those tickets he buys from kids, he has Tom's and the four seats to every game as a School Board member. That's why not."

"No! Does he? I had no idea."

"Of course. But that's merely the start of it. Don't you know how the system works? Every fall the school people send out tickets free. The newspapers get theirs, even the business manager grabs off a couple, the presidents of the banks, and all the prominent citizens here in town."

"They do? Well, for Pete's sake! D'you suppose Mrs. Shaw knew that when she asked me?"

"Oh, I daresay not. The men keep these things to themselves. It's a form of polite graft. Anybody who wants to go goes. Those who don't can always get rid of seats for the Semifinals or the

Finals for a matter of twenty to thirty bucks. It's a nice source of income for those who aren't interested in sport. Mind you, these folks get seats in the middle of the floor in the front row. Even some of the families of the boys who play on the team have to sit up back in the bleachers. But I'd like to bet you'll find J. Frank and Harry Benson and Fred Rogers and the really important men in this town in the front row on Saturday at the Coliseum. As for the kids in the high school, they sit on the ends. Or anywhere at all. They tell me seats are selling in the factories for twenty-five bucks. It's a racket, that's what it is."

The word "racket" had a sinister sound as he rolled it in his mouth.

"You mean to say these people don't even have to pay for these seats they get?"

"Of course not. If they're on the list."

"How do they get on the list in the first place?"

"The Superintendent of Schools tends to that. He darn well knows which side his bread is buttered on. The way it works out is that the kids have nothing to do with their own game. Except the five who play for the pleasure of the older folks and the couple of hundred who are admitted to cheer."

"This girl, now, this Betty Jane Emerson, put it pretty good. She said basketball would be all right if it weren't for the older people. She's a kid that got left out and wants to go. I'm trying to get her a seat."

"Great!" His eyes lit up. "Kids are wonderful, aren't they, Don? They think straight on things; they cut out the non-essentials and get right down to bedrock. That's really good, that is. Let me see now, what can we do for her? She simply must go to that game on Saturday if she feels this badly. By heaven, it's her team, not J. Frank's."

"Funny. I came on her crying in the corridor of school just now. And she said the same thing. Only she said it this way, 'It's my team, not theirs.'"

"There you are again. They sure think straight, don't they? Wonder what it is that changes us into fuzzy thinkers as we grow older. Well, now, let me think a minute. I don't get any newspaper seats, because, of course, I'm not on their list. But . . ."

"You know, Peedad, what I'm afraid is that the Principal won't have any seats left tomorrow. It's the day before the game."

"Hold on a minute." He yanked open the top drawer of the ancient desk. "They don't send any to the paper; but, by ginger, they can't keep my four tickets as a member of the Board away from me. I always hand them over to some boy or girl who wouldn't otherwise get to go. This time . . . I think I gave two to young Dick Hartley . . . two seats . . ." He fumbled through the drawer, upheaving papers, envelopes, matches, bills, pencils, erasers, a couple of rubber stamps, and several dozen other miscellaneous objects. "I recall I gave Dick two, and I should have two more in here . . . somewhere . . . no . . . yes, sir. Here they are! There! Take 'em down and give 'em to that girl. Tell her she's quite correct, that it's her team, not theirs."

The little man stood and stuck out his hand. It was the fist of a fighter, lean and hard, not the fist of a jailbird. Don began to wonder whether someone wasn't mistaken in the things that were said about the editor of the *Evening Press*. He certainly didn't talk like a criminal or act like one, either.

"Don, I'm mighty glad to be able to help. Come up and see me again, real soon, too."

"I sure will. Good-bye, and thanks lots. She'll

appreciate this, Peedad." He turned, went out, and down the stairs two at a time, as he had gone up. But there was a different feeling in his heart.

In the drugstore below, Betty Jane was finishing her coke. She jumped off the stool as he entered with the two tickets prominently showing in his hand. He glanced up in time to see an expensive ulster coming down the aisle toward them just at the moment when he was extending the two pasteboards to Betty Jane.

The face of the girl as she reached out for the tickets was glowing. Don watched her because he didn't care to watch J. Frank approaching in the rear.

"Good evening, Don!" What J. Frank saw as he went past them was a girl reaching out for two green tickets. They were tickets for the Finals. Everyone in Springfield knew what they looked like. There was ice in J. Frank's tone and ice in his glance as he moved toward the revolving door.

21

One team from the northern part of the state, La Porte; one team from the southern part, Evansville; two from the central section, Springfield and Anderson. Four teams. All that were left of the 778 hopeful squads that began play in the Sectionals exactly one month before. Four out of 778!

Outside the Coliseum the cars were parked in long rows, reaching as far as they could see. Their party turned in the gates, and the cops on duty, seeing the signs on the windshields, waved them past. They drove slowly down the long road past the rows of parked cars. Already the crowd was gathering and numerous people were walking toward the entrance. Someone recognized them.

"Hey, Springfield! Knock 'em dead, Wildcats!"

Slowly they went up to the main gates where half a dozen official cars were drawn up. Beside these official cars were the radio trucks with the names of the stations on each one. Fourteen stations were carrying the Finals that afternoon, and among the trucks was one with a familiar look. Every Wildcat recognized the comfortingly familiar words painted in orange on the outside: STATION WSWP SPRINGFIELD. Buck Hannon, they knew, was already on the job.

Prospective customers swarmed in masses around the entrances, offering large sums for tickets for all three games or only one. And no one had a ticket to sell. Once inside, the hallways were filled. People spilled and jostled each other in the corridors. They held hot dogs in one hand and cokes or cups of coffee in the other. They greeted the team as they went through. "Hey there, Tom! There's

Walt. There's Jim. Hi, Jim!" But the boys hurried along to the dressing room, eager to get ready and into action.

It was a largish room, light and clean, with a metal clothes rack well supplied with hangers at one end. There were the usual benches against the tiled wall and a long table in the center. The light pouring in through the windows made their own small and unventilated quarters in the basement of the Hanson gym seem more antiquated than ever.

Quickly they jumped out of their clothes, whistling, yelling to each other, clapping their hands and singing. Don could see they were still loose, still unaffected by the importance of the contest ahead. His heart leapt. They're good and they know they're good. He appreciated that he was the most nervous person in the room and walked back and forth, vainly trying to conceal his nerves.

"Hey there, Red," said someone from the benches, "gimme some band-aid."

"Anyone got any extra gum? . . . Thanks."

Several boys, dressed save for their sweaters, now began to limber up. Feet wide apart, they leaned over, bending to the floor, then straightening up, arms extended. As others finished dressing, the basketballs began to fly back and forth. Russ Brainerd, sitting placidly on the edge of the table, spoke.

"Careful there, boys, careful there; watch your fingers; not too hard."

Chester Herd, the scout, came over and stood at his side. In undertones they discussed the Anderson team. "Yes, I could tell that when I first saw them play last fall," remarked Chester. "I can always tell what kind of a club it is by where it shoots from. You hafta watch these little peculiarities."

Don stepped forward. "How much time, Russ?" Unable to stand still, he walked back and forth by the table.

"Eight minutes till one."

"All right. O.K., boys." They gathered round, some sitting on the bench, their heads up, their jaws moving. Others stood at the ends. "Put on your sweater, Tom. Don't get cooled off, boy." He stood before them, the chalk, as usual, in his hand.

"Want you to go out there, shoot some long ones, a few short ones, and get the feel of the floor." He tried to toss the chalk with nonchalance in his hand, but it fell to the floor and broke. "You all know their numbers, don't you?

Mac, you're on this Rollins, number 6. We've heard he's sprained a leg muscle, but we don't know for sure. We do know he's fast, even if he isn't right. Tom, you're on Benner; Jim, you're on Davis, number 14."

He bent down on one knee, running the forefinger of his left hand inside the collar of his shirt. "They're good ballhounds, we found that out last winter. They'll score if you don't watch 'em close every minute. They hope to get three on one or three on two. If they succeed, get back, get back fast. And *meet your pass.* Handle that ball, handle it alla time. Watch the ball onto your hands. Catch it before you throw it.

"Walt, keep those hands up every minute, but be careful, boy, don't foul 'em. What's that, John?" The boy mumbled something about the officials. "I know, they've been tough on you, these two men, but never mind; never mind that, forget it. You just go out there and play your game. Mac, keep your hands up on that boy, Rollins. Upset him. Get that ball down. But don't lunge, don't jump at him, or you'll foul and get put out of the game. They'd like for you to lunge; don't do it. Tom, you're captain, you gotta be smart out there; I'm counting on you

every minute. Now then, any questions? O.K.,
go out there and play . . . like . . . you've been
playing since the start of this Tournament."

Clapping, shouting, they rushed for the door,
pushing each other, treading on each other's
heels. Don yanked on his coat and followed them
with quick steps. The crowd in the corridor was
thicker. Carrying basketballs in their hands, the
boys worked their way through.

"Hey! There's Tom . . . hey, Tom!"

"Mac . . . hullo, Mac!"

"There's Springfield now. Yea! Wildcats!"

An Anderson supporter yelled at them in a
high-pitched voice, "You'll be surprised!"

They passed through the crowd and onto the
floor. The Anderson team, already out under the
far goal, looked unusually big and tall as good
teams always do. A shriek rose as with Tom Shaw
leading them the Wildcats jogged onto the floor.
The Springfield stands rose.

"Yea! Wildcats! Yea! Wildcats! Fight-team-
fight!"

Standing, yelling, the Springfield crowd continued to shout.

"Hullo, Red!
Hullo, Blue!

Hullo, Team!
We're proud of you!"

The Springfield section was directly behind
the press box and the radio booth, so that the
announcers, to make themselves heard, were
forced to cup their hands around the microphones. Now the Anderson side responded. The
yell leaders, four boys in blue satin suits, ran
out. The roars echoed back and forth across the
floor, continued every second. Their mascot,
the famous Anderson Indian, did a dance
across the floor in full regalia, drawing cheers
from the Redskin sections. The crowd almost
filled the huge arena and was still pouring in
while the Wildcats were twisting and jumping
under the basket. Soon the officials appeared,
one of them with a brand new ball under his
arm. The roar became louder, then suddenly
died away. The players stood motionless as "The
Star-Spangled Banner" was played.

It was over. Each team gathered at the sides.
The Wildcats bent their heads together. Don
leaned over with them, feeling their hot, wet
hands.

"Go out . . . and play ball . . . like I know
you boys can."

The roar, which had risen and risen, suddenly became an intense shriek. The referee in the middle of the floor was holding the ball up, his whistle in the other hand.

Don sank back on the bench. Now it's up to them.

22

Walt MacDonald lay stretched out along the table, while Doc Showalter, the best osteopath in Springfield, felt his ankle. Don stood at one side, Chester Herd on the other, both watching anxiously.

"How's that feel? There?" He twisted the ankle gently from side to side.

"Oh, that feels good, Doc, it really feels all right." The face of the boy on the table, twisted with pain as the ankle moved, told the truth.

The man started to massage the foot tenderly. After a while he took some surgeon's plaster from Don, tore off long strips, and stuck the ends to the edge of the table. Then he placed a huge wad of cotton under the boy's instep and carefully taped up and around the injured ankle. Gradually the boy's face relaxed; the pained expression disappeared.

Don glanced at the Doc. The big man shrugged his shoulders and raised his eyebrows. Maybe! Maybe not!

Shoot! To have that happen just when we were hitting on all six. Shoot! To have that happen now. Don turned away to conceal his anxiety. Walter as a guard was not a high scorer. But he was dangerous if ignored, as he often was, by players guarding Tom. It was Walt's icy coolness and sticky defensive play which made him the balance wheel in the Springfield machine.

The boys were walking across to the watercooler, rinsing their mouths and spitting out the water, dashing it on their hot faces. They came back to the bench, drying off their shoulders and necks, heaving and puffing, heads down. At last one or two began to talk in short, jerky sentences about the game.

"Well . . . what of it?"

"I said they can't score, can they?"

"Yeah, Jim, but you gotta watch him just the same."

"He's fast, he's dangerous."

"Aw, Tom has him bottled up. Gee, Tom, you were great out there!"

"Naw . . ."

Don intervened as they argued up and down the bench. "Now . . . now . . . sit back and relax, relax, everyone. How's it feel, boy?" Walt rose from the table, stepped down, and gingerly put his weight on the injured ankle. He nodded, walked a couple of steps toward the window, returned to the bench and, taking a towel from Red Crosby, sat down, mopping his neck and face.

I wouldn't feel safe if we were 12 points ahead. Well, we are and I don't! Don recalled his words to the sportswriter in the gym earlier in the week. If only they don't get overconfident. If only they don't grow careless and start throwing that ball around. If only they don't let that lead melt away as it did against Fort Wayne.

He knelt down and chalked the usual diagram on the floor. Then he took the scorebook from

Russ and read briefly. "Little has two. Tom has one. One on Jim and one on Walt. Now, boys, that 17 to 5 score doesn't mean a thing. Not one thing. Remember what happened over at Muncie last week. Let's us score right at the start, this quarter. If they get to picking you out there, work that ball . . . work it. When they pick you, John, roll away from that guy. Roll away from him, like this." He shifted his torso with a quick step or two, rolling his shoulders away from them. "Get it? See what I mean?"

"Tom! You must keep after 'em every minute; you tell 'em; don't allow 'em to get lazy on you. No one can be a lazy defensive player and keep position. Can't be done!"

"Three minutes, Don," said Russ in the rear.

"No laziness now! Wait until you work into position to shoot. Don't throw until you see a man's hands in the clear. Tom, he just lobs that ball up there, just lobs it up. John, don't quit on those fouls, boy. Make sure you hear the whistle. Once or twice that second quarter you thought you heard it and stopped cold. It like to cost us a couple of points. Be sure you hear the whistle. Walt, how's it feel now?"

The boy raised his head and nodded. "Just fine."

"Good! This is the bread-and-butter quarter. If you play like you know how to play, it's in the bag. Let's us outscore them in this quarter about 8 to 3. Remember, because you're out in front is no excuse for wild shots. No excuse whatever. All right. Use your ingenuity . . . and go!"

In the maelstrom of excitement that beat around his ears, Buck Hannon at the radio bench tried to explain to the listeners at home what had happened. And just how it happened. His was a difficult task. Although he wore no hat, a sports shirt open at the neck, and a light sports jacket with no vest, he was hot. Perspiration poured down his wide face as if he had been playing. He had been playing. For Buck was not an impartial sports reporter. He was a Wildcat fan from Springfield. Like every Wildcat rooter, he suffered and fought with the players on the floor. At the moment his expression showed his suffering.

As he talked into the microphone, shrieks, whoops, whistles, war cries, and cheers came from above and around, echoed and re-echoed across the floor. The Coliseum was an orgy of emotion, wild, untamed. In front of his machine, cheerleaders of both sexes turned handsprings and somersaults. And all the time people on both sides and behind jostled and pushed and shoved and thumped poor Buck on the back in frenzied excitement. While throughout the quarter he had to sit watching Anderson slowly eat into the Wildcat lead.

". . . And there's the whistle, folks." He nervously mopped his face. "Now let me tell you what happened in that important third quarter. Coach Miller of the Redskins, realizing his star, Rollins, was in no shape to compete, yanked him after that first half and sent in Billy Erskine. Up to this point Springfield was plainly the better team. This boy Little was an elusive, deceptive forward, taking that shovel pass from Shaw and going in there to score time and again. Shaw was the best man on the court, good for the rebound under *both* baskets, under the Anderson goal and under his own, too. Together with MacDonald, he was stifling the Anderson offense. Then Walt fell and injured that ankle. And in the third quarter, when this boy Erskine came in, the Redskin offense began to click. He really went to town; he started to pour it on. The Indians got to rolling and scored five straight points, making the score . . . 17 to 10, for our boys. The Wildcats got a little rattled as Anderson overhauled them, as the Indians chopped down that big lead. They began to chuck those long ones, exactly as they did last week against Fort Wayne. Then York slipped in a couple of lucky one-handers, cutting the lead down some more, in just about the craziest rally we've ever seen in State Tourney. Now, with the whistle blowing for the last quarter, the score is . . . Springfield Wildcats, 21; Anderson Indians, 19. 21 to 19 in favor of the Wildcats."

Out on the floor the team stood in a circle. One or two had their arms on each other's shoulders. Their mouths were open, their faces flushed and red; sweat poured off necks and shoulders. They shifted uneasily on their feet as they looked back toward the bench.

Don shook his clenched fist at Tom Shaw. There's the kid that can spark 'em. Get in there, get in there and fight, said his fist. The big boy saw him and responded with a nod. All through the quarter Don had died a thousand deaths as he watched that lead disappear. They'll never learn, will they? You tell 'em; you tell 'em and tell 'em. But they still have to learn the hard way.

Directly before Buck Hannon, and greatly to

his annoyance, four Anderson cheerleaders took the floor. They wore elegant satin suits of red with an Indian head in green on each chest. Two of the boys had on green trousers. They called for a yell from the crowd, and spelled out the team's name.

"ANDERSON. FIGHT-FIGHT-FIGHT!" Across the floor, the Wildcat yell leaders danced out and called for a reply.

"Yea! Wildcats! Yea! Wildcats! Wildcats . . . Wildcats . . . Wildcats!"

Meanwhile, down in the front row, J. Frank Shaw turned to the man at his side. "See? Whad' I tell you? It's that guard who's slowing them up. He hurt himself the time he fell last quarter. Watch him now when they call time. See? He's limping. See there! They're getting round him every play. They'll lose if Don keeps him in the game."

"Why doesn't he throw in a sub?"

"You know why; hasn't got one."

"Yes, but a poor sub is better than an injured regular any day."

"Of course. This man Miller knows that; he took Rollins out and the Indians started to click. See . . . another foul . . . shows the team is disorganized."

The tall Anderson boy stepped to the foul line. He made it and a roar rose above the arena. Over the center of the floor the four-sided electric scoreboard blinked furiously. "SPRINGFIELD 21 ANDERSON 20." The worst of all scores at the worst moment of the game. Six minutes to go, less than six minutes in the last quarter, and the other side only a point behind.

"We'll win . . . we'll win . . . by golly, we'll win!" shouted the Anderson stands as the teams lined up for a jump ball. Now they were separated by only a single point. Then, in trying to slow up a fast break by the Anderson forwards, Jim hooked the man with the ball. The toss was good and the score was tied for the first time. The Anderson fans, seeing victory ahead, exploded.

But Springfield responded to the challenge. Rather Tom did, breaking away with desperation, his long body guarding the ball down into the corner. There he faked several times, pivoted, and shot from the side. 23 to 21 for Springfield. Seconds ticked off, minutes went by, the game's end drew closer, closer, closer. But the Indians weren't licked. They roared down the court and, after considerable passing, Erskine raced in to sink a one-hander and even the score.

Seconds later a foul was called on Little, and for the first time in the game the Wildcats were behind—24 to 23.

"Hit 'em again, harder . . . harder . . . harder . . . hit 'em again . . . harder . . . harder . . . harder . . . hit 'em again . . . harder!" yelled the Anderson stands. Springfield took a time out as the crowd, delirious with excitement, shrieked above them. They stood with their arms on each other's shoulders, Tom in the middle.

"There, you see!" J. Frank turned to the man at his side and there was a note of triumph in his voice. "What did I say? I always claimed he was far too young, I claimed that from the first. I wasn't wrong, either. Hasn't had the experience. In this game it isn't enough to develop five players; a coach must have replacements. Why, he's killing those boys! If he'd taken Walt MacDonald out and slapped in a good sub, he might have won. Not now."

Many in the crowd agreed. To many in the stands Springfield was as good as beaten. Not to the Wildcat boys and girls in the section behind the radio men. Nor to Don, sitting grim-faced on the bench. Nor yet to the weary boys themselves on the floor.

"Anderson, fight-team-fight!"

The boys on the floor lifted their heads. It was fine to be in the stands, sitting and watching. But it was different on the court. It was another thing out there dodging the groping hands, evading the hips and shoulders that bumped and jarred you and hurt every time you made contact. It was different when you were behind for the first time in the game. When it was up to you.

Their feet were hot and sore, their legs were rods of iron, their thighs ached with every step, their lungs were leaden bellows that crucified them each time they pounded up the boards. They were through; they were beaten; they were finished. They couldn't; not any more.

Tom waved his fist in their faces. "Gonna quit, are you? Gonna quit, you guys . . . just when we have it . . . won . . . almost . . . gonna quit on Don . . . a fine gang you are . . . a fine team . . . call yerself Wildcats! C'mon, now . . . let's give it all we got!"

Eleven thousand anxious faces watched as the ball rose in the air, fell, rose again and, tapped by Tom's long arm, fell over into John Little's hands. The Wildcats, clawing their way back, were still in the game.

Desperate but cool, exhausted but game, they

raced down the floor, showing what made them dangerous, proving why they had come up, slowly, the hard way, to be veterans of the game. Now they were the Wildcats once more, poised and angry, lips tight, faces set. Now it was firewagon basketball, chances taken, wild recoveries made, spills and tumbles and falls all over the floor, with the outcome of the contest and the Tourney, too, yet to be decided. From the sidelines, as they raced toward him, Don heard what the crowd could not; their quick, sharp breathing, the stream of commands from Tom that held them together, his orders, appeals.

"C'mon, you guys, c'mon . . . fight, Wildcats . . . get in there and fight . . . watch out, Chuck . . . now . . . throw it . . . watch him, Jim . . . follow in, follow in, Mac . . . hey, look out, Walt . . . chuck it now . . . chuck it . . . fight, you guys . . . fight, Wildcats!"

Then suddenly he broke in with his specialty, leaping high off the defensive bankboard to take the ball in the air as only he could do. Down he came with the leather in his hands, turned, twisted, evaded the restraining arms, and passed over to John. The play and interplay of twisting bodies swept down the floor, the five Kats work-

ing in steadily toward the opposing goal. End-
lessly the ball went round; to John, who was
bottled up, to Jim, who couldn't break through,
back to Tom, to Jim, and back once more to
Tom. He tried hard to feint, to get loose for a
shot, but the Indians were watching every gesture. Then from the corner of his eye he saw
Walt standing beyond the ring of enemy players,
alone in the rear.

It flashed through his weary brain. The play
that comes up only once or twice in a game, if
at all. He turned, pivoted, and taking the ball
behind his back made a sudden two-handed flip
over the head of his opponent whose arms were
extended before him. It fell onto Walter's chest.
Thousand percent MacDonald! The boy stood
coolly for a second, some fifteen feet from the
basket. Taking plenty of time, he threw. The
ball never even touched the rim as it went in.

And Springfield was leading by a point.

Only a minute, less than a minute to play.
Now the effect of the long, stern chase began to
tell. Anderson was weary and for the first time
showed it. It takes it out of a team to come from
behind, to work ahead, and then to lose the lead.
They began lunging; there was a scrimmage, and

John, grabbing the ball, was knocked to the floor and fouled. He rose and stepped to the line, that mark which seems so near the basket when you are up in the stands and is really so many yards away when you stand there by yourself, when your team leads by a single point in the final seconds of the game; when everything depends on your reflexes and your nerves; when 11,431 people in the stands above are howling in your ears; when you're out there on your own; when it's up to you.

Unmoved by the steady roar, John took the ball and bounced it twice. The arena stood, shrieking, as he bounced it again, tossed it, and sank the basket. 26 to 24 for the Wildcats.

There were fifty seconds left to play. Now forty seconds. With only twenty seconds to go, Jim fouled York, but Anderson refused the penalty and took the ball out of bounds. There was time for a single shot only, a long heave that bounced harmlessly off the board. The game was over.

They swept into the dressing room hugging each other madly. It was over at last. Tom, the sweat running from his face, stretched out at full length on his back upon the table in the center. Yells, shouts, muffled cries, the slaps of bare hands on bare flesh echoed and re-echoed from wall to wall. Once more the Wildcats had come through.

"Hurry up now . . get those wet clothes off, boys. We've got a job to do tonight, don't forget it. If that La Porte team brings these boys down, we gotta be careful."

No one paid attention. They refused to be worried in their hour of triumph. La Porte or Bosse of Evansville, it was all the same to the Wildcats. They had met the hardest challenge of the year, met it head-on and turned it back. They were confident now, and in his heart Don was confident, too. It was hard not to be confident with that gang out there wearing the Springfield colors.

The Principal, several teachers, Dick Lewis, and one or two fathers of the boys came into the room. Doc Showalter kneeled down to undo the tape on Walt's ankle, as the place resounded to the sounds of running water, to yells, shouts, laughter.

"Tonight, kid . . . tonight!"

"Whoopee, tonight!"

"Boy, are they wild up there in Springfield right now! Are they crazy up there now," said

Dick Lewis. "The kids who couldn't get down to see the game are going mad up there."

"Are they really, Dick? What's doing up there?"

"Are they wild! The kids have collected material for two big bonfires, one at the outskirts of town on Route 20. The school band will meet you there and take you in. Deke Noble's all ready to shoot with a special edition the moment the score is flashed, and the mayor's gonna make an address, and I don't know what all. I bet they just about throw that town in the river tonight."

"That's if we don't throw it in first."

"Right, we'll throw it in first."

"Yea! Wildcats! Yea! Wildcats!"

"Hoo-ray for Walt . . . hoo-ray for Walt!"

"Hoo-ray for Jim . . . hoo-ray for Jim . . . someone in the bleachers hollered . . . hoo-ray for Jim."

"Hoo-ray for Tom . . . hoo-ray for Tom . . . hoo-ray for Tom . . . he's a darn nice guy!"

23

C hester Herd came rushing into the dressing
room, breathless from dodging the mob in
the corridors outside.

"Hey! Doc Storrs is at the main entrance.
Wants two tickets. Any of you boys got a ticket?"

Doc Storrs was the town's most popular and
most prominent dentist. Everyone knew the Doc,
a great fan. Instantly several boys reached inside
their jackets.

"Here ya are, Chester."

"He can have mine."

"Mine, too."

The boys had all been given their seats for the evening game in case they were beaten in the afternoon. Most of them, in the excitement of victory, had forgotten all about their tickets. Chester took two seats and counted out the purchase price.

Of course! Why not. They've done it before against harder clubs. Of course they can.

"Tonight against Evansville we'll play a man-to-man defense. They use Howard, number 11, at center; Schneider, number 6, and Kates, number 14, at guards. We'll start with John on Thompson and Jim on Carter, number 12. D'you all know their numbers? Good! Now, this boy Kates. This is good, unquestionably . . . *if* . . . you don't hold your position. Remember, he'll get an inch on you alla time, Mac; work on him every second. You be in position and make him turn the corner. He's sneaky, he's awful fast. Whatever you do, keep your eyes on that ball. He'll do an awful lotta dribbling, so watch him . . . he likes to catch the ball, throw up his empty hand like this . . . and then throw the other way with his right hand. It's a trick; watch him, Tom!"

He rose, walked back and forth silently, sat on the edge of the table. The chalk crumbled in his hand. "If you work that ball, you can't get hurt." One boy on the bench suddenly jerked up his hands. His chin lifted in an involuntary spasm, showing the strain he was under.

They're as tight and nervous as I am, thought Don. "Now, before the game, get a little rosin on your hands and shoes. Tom, you remember this Kates. He does lots of faking, takes that ball and shoots quick, awful quick. And he likes to cut in here . . ." He leaned over the chalked diagram on the floor. "Howsat, Russ?" he called over his shoulder to his assistant. "What? Oh, yes, I remember now. He buckets offa Thompson. Watch him. When he comes in here, make him turn to the outside, make him turn outside."

Again he stood up, walked around with short steps, now facing the row of boys on the bench, now talking to them with his back turned. Suddenly he whipped around.

"Tom! You gotta rebound. You *gotta* go. If we're off our defensive bankboard, go! Take charge! Take charge in the opening minutes. You be the boss, set the tempo. Fake these boys . . . fake 'em to death . . . then go wide so they can't call you for charging. No fouls. No fouls; hear that, John? And move that ball! Move it! Change your positions a lot."

So much he wanted to say, so much he wanted to tell them. This was the last chance and he found it hard. "Well, boys, we've come a long way, a long, long way. I'm honestly not surprised. I always had confidence in you . . . even back there when no one else had. I still got confidence in you this evening."

The benches scraped on the floor. They rose, hands clapping, shouting, eager to get out and find release in action. "Le's go . . . le's go!" Together the Wildcats trooped through the door.

The two teams contending for the title covered the floor of the arena when Don came out, Bosse at one end, his boys at the other. Two teams left; two out of 778.

And I brought them along, he thought; I stayed with them when the town laughed; I encouraged them and believed in them. And still do.

The crowd was shrieking from every side. The Springfield stands were yelling for their victorious five.

"Fight-Fight, Wildcats . . . Fight-Fight, Wildcats . . . Fight-Fight, Wildcats . . . Fight-Fight!"

He edged in beside Russ on the bench. The

referee passed him and stepped upon the floor with a brand new ball under one arm. He walked slowly in to the center circle and stood fingering his whistle. After a while he looked over at Don and held up a couple of fingers. Two minutes left. Get ready.

The team, his Wildcats, came toward the side. Together they all leaned over, clasping hands as they had done before every game since that early disastrous start. Impossible to say what he wanted. Just time for a clenching of grips, a muttered word or two.

"Go get 'em, team!"

The Wildcats took the floor for the last game of all.

Don sat back on the bench. His head was slightly lowered, his hands tight on his knees as he watched them take position. This was what made coaching so wonderful. So awful, too. It was giving to kids, giving them everything you had, your experience, your knowledge, your life, yourself. Then sending them out into the world while you sat and looked on and suffered with them and for them.

The whistle blew. The ball rose in the air. Tom's giant arm reached high.

Now it was up to them.

24

The Wildcats, as usual, were off from the whistle. Jim grabbed the tip and the team raced down the floor for the initial try. Over to Tom, to Walt in the corner, over to John, who had the easiest of shots right under the basket. He missed and the ball rolled out of bounds. Evansville came down the floor, and Carter hit to make it 2 to 0.

Then Walt fouled Howard who scored quickly to make it 3 to 0. Bosse retrieved the ball, there was a scrimmage, and Jerry Kates, weaving his way in, hit again. Bosse 5, Springfield 0.

Oh-oh, this is bad. The thought came simultaneously to Don and Russ on the bench, to Buck Hannon behind his mike, although he refrained from saying so over the air. This is different. This is the first time they haven't gone into the lead from the start.

Buck had hold of the mike as if it were a baseball bat. The sweat already was pouring from his forehead. ". . . Is fouled by Howard of the Bulldogs. We'll have one free throw, then . . . and there it is . . . the first Wildcat point of the game. Score: Bosse 5, Springfield 1. Mac brings it in . . . there's a tie-up under the basket now, the referee is separating them, and it'll be a jump ball between Shaw and Carter . . . a jump ball . . . and there goes Kates again, a great little player, this Kates . . . he goes down fast . . . a pass to Schneider . . . he takes a shot . . . he shoots from way out . . . he misses . . . the rebound is taken by Tom Shaw of Springfield off the bankboard."

"Old fight, Bosse . . . old fight . . . Bosse . . . Bosse, fight-fight-fight!"

"Yea! Wildcats! Yea! Wildcats! Team-team-team!"

Springfield rallied momentarily to score a foul and a field goal, making the score 5 to 4; but again Kates got free on a fast break and went under with a hook shot to put Bosse ahead by three points. Don's face twisted with anxiety as he watched that elusive rascal he knew so well weave his way through their defense. The boy ran over the ball, head down, dribbling so close to the floor it was hard to stop him.

Darn it all, this is bad. Seems like we can't do a thing with him, seems like. . .

It was 9 to 6 at the end of the quarter. Springfield was missing badly on many close-up shots. The Bosse stands went wild as the whistle blew. Four boys and four girls in white sweaters led their cheers. They stood in line, each with a hand on the shoulder of the one in front, a boy at each end and the girls in the middle.

"B-U-L-L-D-O-G-S, B-U-L-L-D-O-G-S, fight, fight, fight!"

The second quarter began with the Wildcats taking the ball in, only to lose it again on an out of bounds fumble. Then Carter hit to make it 11 to 6. John retaliated with a bucket and it was

11 to 8; but from then on the Evansville lead lengthened steadily. The Wildcats were shooting two to one but were not hitting, and Bosse behind Kates, their little blond sparkplug, pulled away to lead by 19 to 14. In a few minutes it was 25 to 15. After each Springfield cheer, the Bosse stands would interrupt with derision, howling across the Coliseum.

"Yeah! Wildcats!
Who's gonna lose?
Yeah! Wildcats!
Who's gonna lose? Who's gonna lose?"

Don sat in anguish. If only they'd find themselves; if only they'd play their game, the game they can play. If only they'd begin to shoot like they know how.

Kates was dribbling so close to the floor that the tall Wildcat forwards were unable to break up his game. Don was amazed at the boy's facility, at the ease and coordination with which he swept down the floor time and again. This was the worst of coaching, the supreme agony; to sit and watch and be unable to do anything but suffer.

"He'd better yank MacDonald and quick, if he wants to hold this Kates. He'd better yank that boy and pull him soon."

"Is it his ankle, do you think, Dad, that's slowing him up?" asked Mrs. Shaw in the front row with her husband and four friends.

"Sure! But he never was a good guard. Looka that! See that kid go right in there? See him go in under? If Don only had some good subs . . . if he'd only developed a few subs. Imagine what Denny Rogers could mean to this gang right now. Denny would win that ballgame for 'em, that's all. Someone ought to tell Don to yank that boy . . . see there!"

Jerry Kates squirmed and twisted his way through the Wildcat defense once more. He was so small he was lost from the stands in the forest of tall players. Yet somehow he kept possession of the ball. Dodging, twisting, pivoting, finding openings a larger and clumsier player would have missed, he was continually breaking through. He went down there, he faked, turned his back to the guards around him, suddenly darted past and hit the bucket with unerring aim. Springfield was being outplayed.

"Yea . . . Bosse . . . we want more . . . we want more!"

The Bosse stands screamed and the Bosse bench went wild as the score mounted. Quite evidently the Wildcats were upset. A minute later Jim fouled Kates as he came down the floor. The small, blond star sank the basket, and the half ended with the Kats 9 points behind.

The dressing room was silent when Don entered. No shouts, no yells, no handclaps. None of the usual exuberance. Just a row of surprised and exhausted boys sitting with their heads bowed on a long bench against the wall.

He stood there for a second. Not one looked up.

"Well!" Suddenly he shrieked. "You boys got anything to say?" He turned away in disgust. Still they sat, speechless, motionless, quiet save for the panting and heaving of their chests.

With a quick movement he turned back, looked at them scornfully, and then suddenly grabbed a chair. He raised it above his head and flung it as hard as he could against the opposite wall, ten feet away. It struck with a crash and crumbled into splinters.

Still their heads stayed down.

He walked back and forth, to and fro, half crazed in agony. "You patted yourselves on the back one game too soon, didn't you?" With a savage gesture he kicked the big table in the center of the room. It overturned with a bang. Russ's surgeon's plaster clattered to the floor and rolled across the room.

"I wanna know . . . have you got the guts to come back? *Have you got it?*"

He didn't wait for an answer. He knew no answer was coming. Tugging at his necktie, he yanked the inside of his shirt collar with his forefinger. Still they sat motionless, saying nothing. No one spoke. No one ventured as far as the water cooler, no one cared to watch him in his delirium. "*Now!* Have you got the guts . . . have you?"

He turned to Russ in the rear. "Whatsa score? What? 26 to 17! You play like you were glued to the floor!" Then his voice became a shriek. "*Is there anything I can say'll wake you up? Anything?*"

Not a word, not a sound, not a motion from the bench, save that everlasting panting.

"They shot awful good; but they were in a position to shoot! They were in a position where they *oughta* shoot good." He paused a moment and looked at them. Then he shrieked again. "Who's on Jerry? Who?" He took a suitcase and kicked it so hard that it sailed, as if on skates, across the room. "You won't pass the ball . . . you won't do anything." Back and forth, back and forth across the floor, back and forth he walked. All the repressed feelings and desires of a dozen games poured from him as he yelled at the row of panting kids in uniform. Once more he let go and struck at them.

"Two on one out there . . . two on one . . . and *still* you couldn't score!"

A boy on the bench wiped his face with his arm. But his head hung down. The others sat motionless.

"They haven't got the fouls you have; know why? 'Cause they're really working that ball. *Work that ball. Work it.* You won't pass the ball . . . you won't get in there . . . you won't do anything. Patting each other on the back . . . telling each other how good you are!"

Whenever he paused, silence hung over the room. At his back, beside the pieces of the broken chair against the wall, Red Crosby stood waiting with an armful of towels, not daring to move. No one dared move. Even Russ refrained from holding up his fingers to indicate time slipping past. None of them had ever seen him like this.

"Of course they scored, of course they did!

You played just the way they wanted you to play. Trotting round out there like you were behind a plow horse.

"Cut out that patting each other on the back. Cut it out. Work that ball. *Work it.* You gotta hug that ball alla time." He came closer, flung his coat off, tossed it on the floor behind him. He kneeled down.

"Now here's what you gotta do to win. Here's what you gotta do." Heads came up quickly along the bench.

They watched carefully, listening. Here's what we must do. Now he'll tell us.

He said nothing and again there was that awful quiet over everything. Suddenly he stood up.

"Nope. No, I'm not a-gonna tell you. I've taught you all I can; now it's up to you. You gotta work it out for yourselves. Now it's up to you. Have you got the guts to come back? Have you got the guts, that's all? It's up to you!"

The benches scraped. With one motion they rose and started for the door. No shouts, no yells, no handclaps; no cheers, no crowding and pushing. The Wildcats came out for the last half of the last game. In a different mood.

25

". . . A beautiful field goal by Little . . . a dandy . . . a beauty, making the score 29 to 21 for the Bosse Bulldogs. The score: Evansville, 29; Springfield, 21. What a game this is, folks . . . and here comes Kates . . . that elusive little pepperpot . . . that five-foot-seven package of dynamite . . . he gets in there . . . he's in there . . . he shoots . . . and . . . misses . . . big Tom Shaw has the ball off the board . . . a long pass to Turner down the south side . . .

Jim is directly under the basket . . . *he hits* . . . and the score now is . . . making the score . . . the score now is: Bosse Bulldogs, 29; Springfield Wildcats, 23!

"Here's a time out for Bosse. They're hoping to break up the tempo . . . to stop this last minute surge, this typical garrison finish by the Kats. Let me say, you folks back home in Springfield, you have no idea how mad this place is right now . . . eleven thousand five hundred fans on their feet . . . everyone on his feet yelling . . . as we go into the last five minutes of play. Oh, boy—oh, boy, has this been a ballgame . . . you gotta hand it to these five kids . . . they've put on a great drive . . . you gotta hand it to 'em."

Buck's voice was gone. It was a rasp, a dull bark, a croak which eloquently conveyed the emotion and strain of the struggle. No one wanted to win that game more than Buck Hannon.

On the floor the Wildcats gathered round their weary leader. His tones were almost as croaking as Buck's. "Jim! You're not following through on that reverse. John, look out, boy, you're letting Kates shoot those long ones too often. Hey there, Chuck, watch that shovel pass of Carter's.

Now we're moving; now we're really moving; now we're starting to hit. Stay with it, you guys, stay with it!"

The whistle blew. Another jump ball between Tom and Howard. Fighting the fatigue of his tired body, he threw himself into the air. But the Bosse center was fresher and tipped the ball to Kates, who was off to a fast break. Doggedly, the Wildcats chased him down the floor, determined to prevent a score.

The little chap worked well in, tried to feint with one hand and throw to a teammate with the other, but big Tom was at his side. Unable to make it, he handed the ball to Carter who passed it round, and finally it was tossed back to Kates who instantly turned and threw. The throw was wide. Tom surged under the basket and leaped up for the board desperately. There was a struggle in the air; but he fell to the floor with the ball tight in his hands.

The fall shook him. He rose and staggered a minute before throwing it to Walt, who made a bounce pass to Chuck. Once again they were dangerous, once again they were in there fighting, edging nearer and nearer to the enemy's basket. To John in the corner, who immediately passed back to Jim, then over to Tom. Tom was covered, so he tossed a bounce pass to John who was all set for his favorite shot from the side. He threw, and the ball went in just as a Bosse player hooked him.

Watching the ball, Tom heard the referee's whistle behind him above the noise. The roar died away and the boys stood round uncertainly, and Tom, near the sidelines, caught yet hardly noticed Buck Hannon's husky tones.

"Yes . . . yes . . . he's fouled in the act of shooting by Howard, number eleven on Bosse. And there are . . . I believe . . . I *think* . . . two free throws to come."

They gathered round the free throw zone. Tom stole a glance at the board. 29 to 25. With two and a half to go! That isn't much time; nor much of a margin for them to work on, either. We can do it; we can do it yet. He slapped them on the back; slapped Walt, leaning over exhausted, hands on his knees, and Jim, blinking behind his glasses, and Chuck, worried and anxious, wiping his forehead with the back of his arm. "We can do it, kids, we can do it yet; c'mon, you guys, c'mon now!"

The whole Coliseum rose as the first shot fell

through the hoop. 29 to 26. The ball was handed back by the referee, and John, the coolest person in the arena, bounced it several times on the floor as though he were practicing in their gym at home.

He stood still a moment. Then he bent his knees, came up with the ball, and let go. It plunked into the net. The Kats were only two points behind.

Bosse was smart. Slowly Kates came down past the ten-second line and stood there holding the ball. The Bulldogs were taking their own sweet time, throwing only when necessary, stalling, trying to hold off that desperate Wildcat surge. Suddenly Kates pivoted and darted in. Tom was there waiting for the break, and raced along at his side, half-deflecting the ball in the air. He jumped high and came down with it, rolling and bumping off several twisting bodies. Regaining balance, he passed quickly to Jim Turner. Now! Not a second to waste.

A long pass to John in the corner. They expected it and covered him, so he passed out to Walt, who handed it over to Tom, who raced behind him and cut in. He searched for an opening but was tied up. Then from the corner John dashed around him, went under, reached for the pass, and tossed up a one-hand shovel shot. The ball rose, hung on the rim of the basket. It fell through, and the score was tied. Anyone's game!

There was a violent struggle underneath the bucket for possession of the ball, a struggle which ended in a tie-up between John and Carter of Bosse. The referee separated them, and tossed the jump ball in the air. John tipped it, but Tom, coming in, missed and it bounced off a Bosse man outside. Kates quicky brought it in. To Howard, over to Schneider, down the floor and then back again to Kates. The little, blond chap seemed inexhaustible. He dodged, rolled away from his adversaries, pivoted, as fresh and agile as he had been in the opening quarter of the first game that afternoon. Now he dribbled in closer, stopping suddenly, turning, threatening from different angles. With Tom every step at his side.

Kates tried to throw, saw he was covered, handed the ball to Carter, who turned and made a wild shot from way out. The ball was recovered by Bosse and passed again to Kates. He feinted, dodged, and as he did so Tom slipped and struck him across the arm with his bare hand. Instantly he heard the fatal whistle of the referee. A foul!

Shoot! Of all things, of all times; an accident, too. Slowly they walked in toward the goal, while the blond Bosse star stood on the line, bouncing the ball. Miss, you; miss it; please miss that shot!

He didn't miss. He never did. The ball bounced in and now the Kats were behind again, by a single point.

Tom brought the ball in. He passed to John and the Kats rolled painfully toward the other goal, while time ebbed away and still the issue remained in doubt.

Over to Chuck, who feinted but was covered an unable to get free. Back to Tom who couldn't get set, a bounce pass to Jim, another bounce pass to Walt, who was tied up plenty, so Walt handed it over to Jim, who feinted, and threw to John in the corner. Their favorite play. Tom held up his hands and shouted to worry them. John made a stab at passing to him, pivoted and threw. It was a perfect toss. The ball fell squarely into the net. Now the Kats were leading by a point.

A shriek rose from the Springfield sections as the ball swished through, a spontaneous and almost erotic shriek which even pierced the crowd roar over the arena. Once more the crazy Kats had come from behind. Once again, when the chips were down, they proved why they were there; once more they had grabbed the lead in the last dying embers of the game. The lifeblood of battle ebbed away. Sixty seconds to go. Fifty-five seconds left. Fifty seconds and there'll be a new champion on the floor.

A fever swept the stands. It gripped not only the frantic Wildcat fans but the Boose rooters opposite. It engulfed the thousands who had no sympathies at stake, who, like most crowds, were for the underdog when the underdog was fighting back. Every man, every woman, every child succumbed to the collective emotion which swept the hall. It was a fever, a malady that possessed the entire structure and all the humans within its walls. The place got out of hand. Slowly, only a few at first, then faster and faster, they poured from their seats to stand round the playing surface, yelling at the struggling figures on the floor. A hastily formed cordon of cops, firemen, and ushers knelt with outstretched arms and clasped fists by the edge of the court, trying to contain the mob. Big Buck Hannon and his assistant, unable to see over the heads of those standing before their bench, grabbed the mike with its long cord and trailed out to the courtside, also.

The tension tightened, increased, became taut and unbearable. There was no world but this. Reality was that heated enclosure. Space was the confines of those four white lines. Time was the electric clock overhead. Life was that intense, thrusting surge below.

The final seconds. The last seconds of the game, of the day, of the Tournament, of the entire season. On the floor the ten beaten figures wrenched for victory. Or defeat.

Then he leaped in and stole the ball. With a quick break, the little blond figure was out in the clear, dribbling furiously down upon the goal.

26

No rush for the showers. No shouts, no yells this evening. No yippees and whoopees. No songs, slaps on bare flesh, no bear hugs. No hollering of young voices. No shrieks of joy back and forth. It's quiet in the dressing room of the team that loses.

It's lonesome, almost. The photographers have suddenly deserted them. So have the newspapermen and the agreeable, smiling sportswriters who came to life after their earlier victories. And all those people who somehow managed to get past the guard at the door—when they were winning. They have gone, all of them. They have forgotten the team that lost. They have gone over there, over to the other side of the Coliseum, to the Evansville dressing room. Once this place was crowded after a game. It's empty now and almost lonely.

Over across are noise and cries and laughter. There the boys are singing and shouting and hugging each other. Around their necks they wear the tattered remnants of the nets which hung at each end of the court. They embrace each other; they walk around shaking hands with the older men who flood the room. Up and down the line they yell hilariously, joyously. Someone else has been given the Trester Award. The Trester Award is always given to a player on the losing side. Let 'em keep the Trester Award! This is the thing we've dreamed of. We won, didn't we? We won the State, didn't we? We're the champs, aren't we?

The cameramen stand before them, flashbulbs in hand, pleading. "Just one more shot, boys; just line up there a moment, boys; you, too, please, coach; won't take a second, just one more shot, please; thank you very much, boys."

There is quiet in the dressing room of the team

that loses. No cameramen, no sportswriters, no visitors. No yells, no shouts, no song, no laughter. Only fatigue, intense fatigue, deeper fatigue because of defeat. Victory conquers exhaustion. You aren't so tired when you win; you are exhilarated. Defeat accentuates the agony of sustained physical effort, overwhelms you, beats you down. You are through, you are finished, you are done. You will never recover, never. You don't care whether you do or not.

The five Wildcats sat in despair on the bench. We've lost. We've lost! We can't go home! We can't go back to Springfield. Why, they'll run us out of town. We've lost and we can't go back. They sat huddled together, too tired even to move. Too tired to drop off those stinking, wet clothes, to walk the twenty feet to the showers.

On the other side of the Coliseum are the sounds of running water and cheers and the noise of the conversation of a hundred persons and the tones of a dozen boys shouting to each other. The place is filled with older men. The dressing room of the team that loses is quiet. No one is interested in the losers. They are quickly forgotten. Nice boys. Too bad they couldn't quite make it!

That's how sport is. Sport is crazy, sport is sentimental; but sport is also hard and cruel. Because nobody could possibly be interested in a team that doesn't manage to win. Except one person.

He was a tall, well-dressed man in a double-breasted suit, with an expensive overcoat slung over his arm. He talked his way efficiently past the guard at the door, who hadn't been too busy since the end of the game. He walked into the stillness of the room. It was so quiet he could hear the gasping sobs of several boys bent over on the benches against the wall. He almost walked on tiptoes. He went across to a tired figure, sitting on the edge of the table in the center.

"Don . . . you probably don't remember me. I'm Townsend Bell of Indianapolis. I met you at J. Frank's house in Springfield the night after you won the Regionals at Marion. Remember? Just dropped in to say that the Athletic Association at New Haven has been considering the appointment of a new basketball coach. They want a man who's young, who is successful, and who can teach Indiana basketball at Yale. I think you fill the bill pretty well, and I'm authorized to offer you the job, if you're interested."

27

The car hummed through the darkness. For a long while no one spoke. They sped beyond the city limits, passed Deer Creek and Broad Ripple. At Carmel Don, behind the wheel, spoke to Tom Shaw at his side.

"We'll eat at Westfield."

"I don't want to."

"We'll eat at Westfield."

"Don, the boys don't want to eat. They don't want food this evening, they said. Do you, boys?"

He turned back to the three figures slumped disconsolately on the back seat.

"Naw."

"Not me."

"Nor me."

"There! See Don?"

"We'll stop and eat at Westfield," Don announced to the car. No one answered.

Ten minutes later they stopped before Joe's Lunch in Westfield. The second car, driven by Chester Herd, was right on their heels; and the third, driven by Russ Brainerd and also full, pulled in shortly after.

"Our boys don't want any food tonight, Don," said Russ from the wheel of his car.

"Nor ours, either," shouted Chester. "They all say they can't eat now."

"We're gonna get us some food here." Don's voice was firm. The three cars slowly disgorged their passengers—a beaten basketball squad. They filed into the restaurant and slumped down at the tables. They were gloomy; but they were willing to put off the arrival back home as long as possible. None of them wanted to go home.

Don knew how badly they felt, but he paid no attention. He walked over to the proprietor.

"Those steaks I phoned you for—are they ready yet, Joe?"

"Be ready in three minutes, Don. We was expecting you. Say, that's a mighty tough one you lost, mighty tough, believe me. Everyone was pulling hard for you."

"Thanks, Joe. That's how things are, I guess; someone has to lose. Rush up that grub, please."

Meanwhile, the boys sat at the tables asserting that food was simply out of the question. They didn't want to eat. They wouldn't eat; they couldn't possibly eat anything. Not if it was placed right there, in front of them, they couldn't. Then a sizzling steak, a large steak with French fried potatoes beside it, appeared before Tom. It smelt good. The others watched, not without interest, as a second steak came for John, and then one for Chuck. With huge glasses of milk and plates of bread and butter. They didn't want to eat; obviously no one could eat at such a time. They just couldn't eat. They merely tasted the steaks to be polite, in order not to hurt Don's feelings, because they were there on the table. Suddenly the steaks began to disappear. They vanished down hungry throats. More milk, please. Some more of those French fries. How's that for some more bread and butter? Hey there, Walt, pass the butter, will ya? Gradually the boys found lost appetites.

•

Meanwhile, back in Springfield fires were burning. But not the fires of victory.

Perhaps it would never have happened had the team won. Maybe the whole thing would have become a celebration and reception for the team had they triumphed instead of losing the State. Maybe that surge of high emotion at the Coliseum, which, thanks to Buck Hannon, had penetrated every Springfield home and every Springfield heart that evening, would have spent itself harmlessly in welcoming home the victorious Wildcats. Maybe. Only the Wildcats lost!

At first it was merely the kids; just a bunch of High School boys and girls who during the late afternoon had been gathering fuel for the bonfires, the bonfires of victory. A dozen or more of them listened to the game at a small radio around the counter in the Walgreen store. There was astonishment when Bosse swept suddenly into the lead in the first half; then hopes and high emotion in the second; then reassurance and certainty of triumph when the Wildcats roared from behind. Last of all, there were defeat and bitter, stinging disappointment.

Hurt and stunned, they poured out. Other kids joined them, catcalling and shouting in the warm March evening. There was something mean and cruel in their yelling as they prowled up and down, up and down, restless, uneasy, ready for anything. They yelled to each other in high tones and shrieked across the streets as friends appeared. All the while they went over the contest.

If only we could have held that ball; we shoulda squeezed that ball. If only we'd got one more goal, one more free throw, even. The Kats were tired; you could see they were tired. If the school had been there to support them, if we'd all gone down, if we could have gotten tickets, it would have made all the diff . . .

There wasn't anything to cheer about; no reason to yell or shout, either. But they surged noisily up Superior and down Buckeye, and down Buckeye and up Superior, yelling and shouting all the time. Merchants along the street came to the doorways of their stores, watching.

Meanwhile older men stood on the corners discussing the event that was on everyone's mind—disaster to the Wildcats. Voices raised, they replayed the last five minutes of the contest. Figures lurched from bars and pool parlors on Buckeye Street; more joined them from the taverns along Superior, noisy, excited, angry men who asked each other why the Kats had lost, why they hadn't got the stuff to come through; what happened to 'em, anyhow? These men had all dropped money, a few of them big sums. They were sore.

The knots on the street corners grew larger and larger. So did the parade of boisterous kids. A few boys hesitated beside the loud-tongued men outside the taverns or on the corners of the lighted streets. They heard their high voices, listened to the excited arguments thrown back and forth.

"Frank Shaw's right. He sure knows his basketball, Frank does." "This fella's too young." "He should never have let that colored boy play. It all started back then." "First thing you know, we'll have a colored team representing this town." "A colored team representing Springfield!" "Yeah, ain't that so, Elmer? Ain't that so, Joe? Why, the first thing you know, this fella . . ."

"Yessir, that's correct. Throwing off one of our good boys for a nigger." "Who is this man,

Henderson? Who does he think he is?" "Thinks he's running this town." "Well, he isn't running this town. Nor the colored folks, neither. They're getting mighty uppity lately, you noticed that? They don't know their places like they usta." "Let's do something about it."

"Let's do something." "What'll we do?" "How 'bout that colored boy, the boy who held up two-three women in town last month, snatched their purses, remember? He's out on bail. Ain't no justice in this-man's town." "Let's us get the blighter . . ."

Larger was the crowd, and more vicious now. Older men were in control. It was no longer a bunch of boys and girls from the High School; it was older and quieter and meaner, too. Now the kids tagged along on the edges, watching with wide open eyes, wondering, fascinated, and frightened.

The crowd swept away from the business center of town, into the colored section over on the South Side, over where the streets were full of pot-holes left by the winter storms and many of the lights on the street corners were gone. Half a dozen men started for a car at the curb and began rocking it. Back and forth, back and forth. Over it went with a crash of breaking glass and splintered wood. They ran across the street to upset another, and then another. Dogs scuttled into the darkened alleyways for safety as every parked car became the prey of the mob. People heard them coming blocks away, heard them and knew what it meant; heard the low crowd-murmur from a distance, that terrifying sound of a mob on the loose. They ran inside the little one-story frame houses, putting out the lights quickly, sitting in silence in the small, darkened rooms as the procession passed by outside.

•

Over at Joe's Lunch in Westfield the telephone rang. The proprietor answered.

"Don! It's for you. Hey there, Don, there's a phone for you."

"For me?" But—they had lost, they'd been beaten! If the team had won the State, there would have been a dozen phone calls and a hundred friends waiting for them right there in Westfield. All Springfield would have been on his neck—had they won. But not when you lose. America has no use for a loser. If you lose, folks let you alone. He rose from the table where his food lay untouched, and went over to the telephone beside the wall.

"Hullo?"

"Don! Is that you, boy?"

"Yes. Who's talking?"

"Homer Wilson, Don. In Springfield. I'm in my office right now."

"Oh! Hullo there, Peedad." It was the first thing that had comforted and cheered him since Jerry Kates sank that basket in the final seconds of play. The first time he had felt any warmth inside since that moment. Win, lose, or draw, the little old man hadn't forgotten.

No, it wasn't about the game or basketball. It was something else. "Don, there's trouble here in town. The boys are on the loose. There's been rioting over in the Negro sections, and they're marching on the City Hall to demand that the sheriff turn over that colored boy to 'em. They're threatening to storm the jail if he doesn't."

Don was confused. "That colored boy! What boy?"

"The boy that was caught swiping women's pocketbooks last week. They raided his home; but he was in jail, and the boys are after him."

"But, Peedad, we . . . they . . ."

"Don, get this straight. The boys are ugly tonight, real ugly. There's only one person in town who can stop 'em doing something they'll be sorry for. That's you."

"Me!"

"Yes, you. I want you should jump into the fastest car you got there, and drive like hell for the City Hall. The mayor'll hold 'em outside as long as he can. But you've got to make time. Don, you've got to drive like you never did before."

28

The car raced down the long, flat highway. Farms beside the road stood out in the thin moonlight, their white houses dwarfed by the barns and silos near by. The speedometer steadily at sixty-five, he went straight ahead, on toward Springfield and trouble. Cicero, Arcadia, Atlanta; little, sleepy towns flashed past. He slowed down at Tipton and turned left into the road for home, picking up speed the moment he left it behind. Places he knew came toward him, vanished in the rear, until finally he saw far ahead a gleam of light in the distance.

The light could only come from a bonfire at the junction of Route 20 on the edge of town. Consequently he assumed the trouble must have died down. Very likely things had cooled off; most probably the band would be there beside the fire, waiting for the team, ready to escort them into Springfield. But as he approached the junction of Route 20 he realized the light was not one of welcome. In fact, it was not from a bonfire at all, but from the flaming embers of what a short time before had been a fiery cross.

Peedad's tense tones came to him. "The boys are ugly tonight, real ugly . . ."

He took the short cut toward the center of town. Past the Wire Works and the General Motors plant, into West Mulberry, West Maple, and onto Wisconsin Avenue. He didn't hesitate at the traffic lights as he rounded corners on two wheels. Up ahead was Courthouse Square.

He knew the cars would be parked solidly around the building, so a block away he drew up to the curb and jumped out. As he walked rapidly along the street he could hear the sullen murmur of the crowd. The boys are ugly tonight, real ugly . . .

The lights of the Square came closer. So did the cries of the throng before the courthouse. He turned the corner and saw them out along Indiana Avenue, jammed in on the grass before the building which housed the county jail in the basement as well as the law courts and offices above. They were packed together close up to the steps of the ancient structure. On the top step was a handful of men: the chief of police, the mayor, and the sheriff. The mayor was talking, and Don could see his hands gesticulating before his face; but few could hear what he was saying.

Crossing the street, he noticed a rope and a noose attached to a big tree. Underneath and nailed to the tree was one word: "WARNING." He worked through the scattered men on the fringes and so into the heart of the mob. Someone saw him as he pushed through and yelled his name. Heads turned in his direction. Then a brick hurled through the air and struck the stone pillar just beside the mayor's head. It spattered harmlessly into pieces. A workman in overalls below drew back to throw another, but Don was near enough to catch the thrower's arm as he went past. The brick fell to the ground. Closer to the steps, closer, he shoved his way through the dense crowd and, working loose, jumped up to the top.

As he did so, Peedad Wilson, on the outskirts, went quickly over to a youngster standing across the street. He spoke to the boy, and together they hurried down the block to where his car was parked, talking as they went. No time to lose; not a moment.

Bang! Another brick crashed against the stonework as Don reached the top of the flight of steps. He turned, hatless now, for his hat had fallen off as he pushed through. There he stood, bareheaded beside the mayor. Immediately they recognized him. Someone shouted his name, and a dozen, a hundred voices took it up. For just a few seconds the ugly crowd-noise, which had interrupted the mayor and prevented all save those near the steps from hearing his words, died away.

"So! You call yourselves sports! Tinhorn sports . . . cheap sports . . . that's what you are; all of you!" His sharp tones swept over them, carried to the far fringes of the crowd on the other side of the street; he was angry for the second time that evening and unafraid. They were amazed and astonished at his outburst.

"I just came from the Coliseum down there. And from those boys . . . our boys . . . our kids who gave everything they had . . . and a little bit more . . . every last ounce and then some . . . to lose the State by a single point. Out there fighting Bosse, while you were back here slinging bricks at the mayor.

"Just a bunch of kids with guts; that's all they had—guts. No subs to help out like Fort Wayne, no big reputation like Anderson's, an' no stars like Greentown or Bosse; not one. Nothing but guts. And you guys home chucking bricks at a man who can't throw back! And ganging up on a defenseless colored boy down there in jail. Call yourselves sports!"

The crowd shifted uneasily but stood silent, listening.

"Sure, it was all right early in the year. We were winning then, and you were betting and making money, too. You, Jonesy, and you, Scrapper, and you, Milt Morse, and others I can see here, lots of you. You were back of the team then, when they won for you, when they licked

Marion to win the Regionals, when they whipped Burris at Muncie. Remember the odds that day? I do. One to nine, that was the odds against us; one to nine. You were cheering 'em when they trimmed Fort Wayne, and you probably went out and bet your bankroll on 'em this afternoon. Tonight they played their hearts out, all five, and they lost. So you've quit. One point; one measly point; one bucket and we could have won. One field goal and they'd have brought back the State.

"And the bonfires would have been lighted on Route 20 and down by the Federal Building, too, and the band would have been out waiting for us. For them. Why, they feel so bad, these kids, these kids, they didn't want to come home. They hated to . . . come back . . . to Springfield tonight. They feel they let you folks down. You . . . you cheap sports . . . you tinhorn gamblers . . . here you are, taking it out on a colored boy in jail. They lost. So you're quitting on 'em, quitting cold. You're gonna prove the town's not behind 'em. When we win, oh, sure, that's fine. Not when we reach the Finals and lose by a single point."

A sound came from around the corner of Superior Street. Somehow in the few short minutes at his disposal Peedad had succeeded. It was the sound of a drum—a drum and a cornet. Three kids rounded the corner and came past the Square; three kids, one helping carry the drum. They marched along under the street lights on Indiana Avenue in the rear of the crowd, playing the Wildcat song. Heads turned.

"Fight—fight—Wildcats!" Boom! went the drum. The kids standing on the edge of the crowd, who had heard every word, looked at each other.

"Hey, Sandy! Hey there, Stretch . . . hey, Junior . . . hey, Casey! Let's go. Let's us get the bonfire started. Let's show the team we're back of 'em." They fell in behind their three schoolmates; four or five, six or seven, a dozen, more, and more, singing as the band picked up momentum.

". . . Never stop . . . never quit . . . never fall . . . Fight . . . fight . . . *Wildcats.*" Boom! went the bass drum, as they yelled the name.

"Every sec . . . keep your eyes . . . on the ball . . ."

A few older men swung along with them. Others joined and the column grew, faster and faster. The crowd was now edging away from the steps, away from Don and the chief of police and the mayor and the fragments of broken bricks at their feet on the upper landing. And the noose hanging from the tree.

"Fight . . . fight . . . Wildcats . . ." Boom!

"As we roll . . . toward the goal . . . with a roar . . .

"Fight . . . fight . . . *Wildcats* . . ." Boom! Boom! Boom!

"We . . . will . . . score!"

Down Superior and into Buckeye. The crowd was growing. It reached so far back that the ones in the rear could hardly hear the booming of the drum up front where the kids were. But they could distinguish the cheers, the shouts of the youngsters behind their picked-up band.

Then a small figure in white dashed out, waving a megaphone as big as himself. Deke Noble's youngest boy, one of the cheerleaders, had already returned to town. He raced out before them in his white sweater with the big red S.

"Yea! Wildcats! Yea! Wildcats! Team . . . team . . . team!" It swept up and down the long column; those in the rear yelled back at those in front. "Yea! Wildcats! Team . . . team . . . team!" The procession turned at West Mulberry and moved into Post Office Square. There, before the new Federal Building, was the gigantic bonfire gathered by the students earlier that evening in anticipation of victory. Someone had reached the spot before them. Already it was crackling into flames, throwing a queer light over the white stone structure. Right then the crowd poured into the Square at one end, while at the other two cars drove up with the team.

The Noble boy danced out before his friends. "Yea! Wildcats! Yea! Wildcats! Yea! Wildcats! Team . . . team . . . team!"

Now the paraders broke ranks and surged forward, pressing round the wide steps of the Federal Building, the band still playing the Wildcat song. Then the squad was coming through them and up beside Don on the wide step at the top. He stood quietly, still hatless, the five boys grouped behind him. They looked curiously down at the vast flood of faces in that strange light from the flames of the bonfire. At one side were the familiar countenances of their schoolmates grouped around the little band.

"Attaboy, Tom . . . nice work there, Tom, nice work, kid." "Hey, Chuck!" "Hey there, Walt!"

Why, we didn't know, we didn't realize folks

felt like that . . . we didn't hardly think they'd be glad to see us . . . win . . . lose . . . or draw . . . say, this is great . . .

Don held up one hand. The crowd was tamed now and easy to handle. They kept silent, the drum was stilled, and you heard nothing but a restless movement of bodies edging closer and closer toward the steps and the team.

". . . First, the boy who pulled us through our toughest matches all season . . . who played thirty-two minutes of every game in the Tourney . . . a great competitor . . . a great player . . . and a great boy . . . who won, and I'll say he deserved to win . . . the Trester Award. Our center, number five, Tom Shaw!"

The big fellow with the crew haircut stepped forward. He stood dazed by the noise, by the glare from the fire, by the warmth of their greetings. For the crowd yelled affectionately and kept on yelling, and yelled some more; and as they continued the bitterness of defeat left him. Left the others, also. Then someone smacked the big trophy into his hands, the figure of a basketball player in bronze. He stood with the thing in his arms, not looking foolish or feeling foolish, staring out at them. Then he held it up and waved it at them. They yelled back spontaneously. And little Jack Noble on the edge of the steps danced back and forth.

"Yea! Wildcats! Yea! Wildcats! Yea! Wildcats! Shaw . . . Shaw . . . Shaw!"

29

Don stood looking out the window at the Federal Building opposite. There wasn't much to say.

"Well, Don, I'm sorry you're leaving, mighty sorry to see you go."

"Same here, Peedad. Feller gets to love a place where you struggle and the kids you struggle with, also. I've had some right happy times in this little old town." Some tough ones, too, he thought. Turning from the window, he sat down in the single chair unencumbered by papers, proofs, or manuscripts. The old chap, as usual, had his feet on the desk. Above his head on the wall was a sign.

AIN'T GOD GOOD TO INDIANA

"You know, Don, I still think I could make enough trouble on the School Board to bring you back here next year."

"You could; but it wouldn't be worth the fight. Besides, I've agreed to go to Yale."

"We'll miss you. We need you here in lots of ways. Basketball is too important in this town to have the wrong kind of direction. When a coach is good, the whole set-up in the school is good. When he's bad, well, you remember Mason over at Pottsdown. He had those Gregory twins playing, remember? Whenever one had a couple of fouls slapped on him, Mason would change their shirts between halves. You know all the shady little tricks; kids pick 'em up fast when they see older men use 'em. But if you go, you go, I guess."

"Sometimes I wonder why anyone ever coaches basketball in this part of the world. Springfield isn't the only town hereabouts where men like

Frank Shaw run the School Board the way they want to, and the gamblers meddle with the team, and the pressure groups gang up on a coach when he has a couple of unsuccessful seasons. That's why coaching gets to be a pain in the neck. Sometimes I hardly know why a man sticks at it."

"I'll tell you why, Don. They stick for the excitement and the adventure that's in the game. The pioneering spirit of our ancestors, that's what makes 'em stick. The feel of competition in a man's blood; that's what keeps 'em going. You see, since business has become such a huge, impersonal thing in this nation, with men employed by a corporation and bosses that they never see, with the head office in Chicago or New York or London even, why, sport has become our great national adventure. What does every boy in this town want to be? He wants to be a basketball coach. It's the dream of the U.S.A.; the prairie wagon and the plains; the unconquerable frontiers, the urge and restlessness in every American. That's why you stick it; that's why coaches stay with the game."

"Basketball's wonderful. It does something to a man," said Don thoughtfully.

"I'd agree that basketball is wonderful as long as it's a game. But here, now, in this region, it's a sort of disease. Look what it does to folks. See what it does to our education. A star player fails his mid-years and the businessmen tell the teacher he'd better pass the boy if he wants his contract renewed. So he gives the boy a special exam after school and passes him."

"Not in our school. Not our boys," said Don, with resentment in his voice.

"Shucks, no! Hinton's not that kind of a principal. Besides, you had all A pupils. I'm a-talking about the overall picture of the State, what the game does to folks in this region. Everybody's in on it. The banks buy up the bonds of the Field House and make 6% interest on a sure thing. The merchants in town take in $25,000 on the Saturday of the Regionals. See how it affects the boys, sometimes. Last championship team we had was years ago now. But I recall it went to the boys' heads so that they felt the city owed them a living. They wouldn't work to go to college, they wouldn't take jobs, they wouldn't do anything. Know where they are at present? Five of 'em, all five—day laborers."

"Say! They are! I didn't know that."

"I tell you, basketball's a disease. It corrupts our standards, helps the gamblers chisel in on

a sport, exploits the youngsters for the amusement of older men like Fred Rogers and Frank
Shaw. Why, it even takes a decent citizen like
you and turns him into a raving maniac, smashing chairs and overturning tables and cursing
round, merely because his boys don't run up a
score."

"Oh, no, Peedad, you're wrong; you got me
all wrong there. I didn't mean it that way at all."

"I heard about that scene in the dressing room
at Indianapolis last Saturday night."

"No, no, Peedad, I had to shake 'em up, to
startle 'em, to . . . I had to put on an act."

"Partly. You think now it was an act. We often
think the way we want to, Don. But basketball
did something even to you; it made you lose
control; you got to the end and you let yourself
go; you know very well in your heart you did."

"Yes, but, Peedad . . ."

"Listen. I heard that roar over at the Coliseum
when Springfield took the lead in the last quarter,
toward the end of the game. Don, boy, that's the
same roar exactly we heard here in Springfield
later that night when the boys raided the colored
sections on the South Side. Know what it is?
Lemme tell you. It's the roar of the mob, the

cruel mob, who burn books or houses or humans or anything they can lay their hands on when they're in the mood. That's what basketball can do to folks. As a game it's O.K. Right now, the thing is beyond us, Don; it's out of hand."

"I don't know, I don't hardly know; maybe you're right, Peedad. I never quite thought of it that way."

"Think I am. Don, Indiana's a grand State. You know, we have more lawn mowers per capita than any other State in the Union. That says something about us. It's the Middle Land; we don't get so excited about most things as folks do on the coast—on either coast. But we live in this great big round world, Don, and we can't hardly escape what's in the air we breathe, what's happening every place. Folks here are the same fundamentally as other places; when the ugly spirit of the mob seizes them, they get out of hand same as everywhere else."

"This basketball . . . I wish . . . I don't really know . . . I'm sorry, Peedad, I'm going to Yale."

"Yes, I'm sorry, powerful sorry. We'll all miss you here in town. There's a few folks that hate you right now will be wishing to high heaven you were here, come next winter. We'll miss you all right, and I'll miss you most of all."

"Peedad, before I leave and while I think of it, I'd like to ask you a kinda personal question, something that's been puzzling me for quite some time."

"Go ahead, Don, go right ahead."

"It isn't true, is it . . . that you were ever in jail?"

"You've been talking to your friend, Frank Shaw, haven't you, Don? Why, yes, it's perfectly true."

"Oh!" There was disappointment in his tones and in his heart, also.

"Here's the facts about that, Don. I exposed the sewerage scandal in the *Press* about four-five years ago and told the whole story. Named some names, too, because I had the dope in my files. The boys along Superior Street, the bankers and your friend, Frank Shaw, thought they saw a chance to put me out of business. They sued and had Judge Davis put bail at $10,000. I just couldn't raise the cash then because things were mighty tight and all the bankers in town were Frank's friends. They wouldn't help."

"What happened? How'd you get out?"

"Sam Silverman."

"Sam Silverman! You mean Silverman, the junk dealer, that Jewish feller?"

"That's correct. He was the only person in town to ride along with me. Silverman came to the jail and said, 'Here, Peedad, I guess you might need some money.' And he handed me an envelope with ten thousand dollar bills. Wouldn't even let me give him a note! Just said, 'Why, Peedad, I know you. It isn't likely you'll be leaving town in a hurry.'"

Don whistled. "Golly, that's different. I didn't hear it quite that way. What finally happened?"

"I fought the case all the way up to the Supreme Court at Indianapolis and beat 'em every time. It took every cent, everything I had invested in the paper, all my wife's money; but I finally won."

"Oh! I see! I didn't realize . . . I didn't know." Now he understood the small office, the dingy room, the shabby little man for whom he felt more respect. Yes, there were lots of things about Springfield a fellow had to learn.

"Don, there's a heap of things under the surface here-abouts. You'd get on to 'em fast enough if you stayed. I wish you would, I sure wish you would. The young men don't seem to stay. Remember what Plutarch said? 'As for me, I live in a small town where I am willing to continue, lest it grow smaller.'"

"Yeah, I know, Peedad, I know. I'm sorry, too, in a way, but I've agreed to go to Yale."

"Our young men all fall into three groups. The best ones, the bright ones, the keen ones move away. Then there are those who stay and play ball with Frank Shaw and the boys along Superior Street. The few left in the third group try to fight, but they're licked from the start, and there aren't many of them. If you won't work along with J. Frank, you can't even get credit at the banks—don't I know it! Don, I wish the worst way you wouldn't leave. You know, you're the one most important person in Springfield, Indiana, right now."

"Why, Peedad, what on earth makes you say that?"

"Because you are. You have the most influence of any man in town; more'n any editor, more'n any preacher, more'n the chief of police, more'n the mayor, even. You saved us from a race riot last Saturday night when the mayor and just about everyone else had failed. Everybody in town knows you and nearly everybody likes you, too. I wish you'd stay, here . . . with me."

Don was startled. "With you?"

"Yes, right here. On the paper, working with me. There wouldn't be so much money. Lots and lots of work; a good many heartaches and disappointments, too. But, Don, you're the one man we have who can really lead. It's a funny thing; the kids all have a kind of emotional investment in the basketball coach here in this section. D'ja ever notice they call you Don? They don't ever call a teacher in school by his first name! All this, all the idealism of America, is in these basketball kids, and it's what they devoted to you. 'Course . . . I know some folks sneer and laugh when you say ideals. I don't. It's what made America. It's what made us different from Europe. The people who came over here were largely idealists; otherwise they'd have stayed put."

"Yes, sure. But, Peedad, I don't hardly see how . . . I don't believe I understand quite what you mean."

"Wait a minute. Here's all that youthful idealism focused on this thing we call basketball; and on you as the leader. Now, Hitler took this and channeled it into something evil and foul. Why don't we channel it into something good? Into constructive outlets? Why do we build it up that way and then let it die? Why do we?"

Don was uneasy. He glanced at the little old

man with the graying hair, an old chap with the seat of his pants worn thin by rubbing on the seat of the ancient swivel chair before the desk; an editor; an impractical old geezer. It was strange how folks in town all laughed at Peedad Wilson. Yet whenever there was trouble in town, like last Saturday, they turned to him and not to J. Frank Shaw who ran the place. And, as Don knew, a thousand people in town loved him for one that loved Frank Shaw. Yes, it was quite true that they laughed at him along Superior Street, but they called him "Peedad." They called Frank Shaw "J. Frank" in quite different tones.

All this made him uncomfortable. Once or twice J. Frank had made him uncomfortable, but not in the same manner.

"Y' see, boy, here's the whole darn thing. This force, this spirit is turned toward you. Then, bang, all of a sudden it vanishes. Why should it disappear? You took the team into the State; you're the most powerful person in town, the one who can lead. You proved it plain enough on Saturday. Don, look; you love these kids; you'd enjoy working with them, working with the Wildcats, for Springfield, now wouldn't you?"

"Yes, think I would. I would . . ."

"You can, if you really mean it."

"How?"

"Stay right here in town with the Kats."

"I can't, Peedad. Not fighting and scrapping with J. Frank all the year. I can't do . . ."

"I don't mean as coach of basketball, not at all. I mean right here, with me. Look, Don, Lincoln came from a town about this size with the same name, a town just over the State line a piece. You and I together make a tough pair; we're fighters, both of us. We might even make this a decent town; not what it is now but a city good enough for Lincoln. It could be done and inside of five years or less you might be mayor."

"Mayor! Mayor!" He laughed. "That's a hot one. That's funny, Peedad. I'm no politician, you know that."

"All the better. What's funny about it? Lots of basketball coaches have gone into politics in this State before now. Maybe that's all the better if you aren't a regular politician; maybe that's why you ought to stick around and make a name for yourself here in town. Ever hear of a man named William Allen White? Well, he was the editor of a small paper over to Emporia, Kansas. He could have made a fortune if he'd gone to New York or Chicago and been swallowed up by one of those big outfits there. But he stayed and made a name for himself, a name that men respected all over America, and folks really loved him, and when he died the nation flocked to his grave. Who you think flocks to the grave of one of those big syndicate men, of those big newspaper executives in New York?"

"I'm sorry, Peedad, but I've agreed to go to Yale."

"They won't hold you to it. Don't quit on us, Don. Stay here. Just think what'll happen to America if all the fighters leave the small towns. Stay and scrap it out with the Wildcats, the Wildcats coming along for years and years."

This was too much. Don rose, grabbed his hat. He went to the door overlooking the dusty staircase. The little room seemed dingier and grubbier, yet more attractive than it ever had before.

"If you change your mind, Don . . . if you'd care to think it over, you might change your mind."

Don was going down the stairs and into the street, across from the Federal Building where the crowd had received the Wildcats home from the State. "If only I hadn't agreed to go to Yale!"

30

D on slapped the last suitcase shut and looked
round the room, thinking that the leaving
was harder than he' had imagined. There was a
knock at the door. Outside stood Tom Shaw.

"Hi, coach!" The serious face of the boy was
more serious than ever as he glanced about the
room and saw the suitcases on the chairs. "You
really leaving? You really mean it, don't you?"

"I'm afraid so, Tom. I appreciated what the
boys all said at dinner last night; but there's a

lot of things happened this year in town which make it better for me to clear out. There ought to be a new deal at the High School, another man down there at the Hanson Gym, someone who can make a fresh start . . . someone without any enemies."

"I don't know any enemies you have at school, Don."

"Sure I have! Tim Baker, and then last year there was Denny Rogers and all his gang."

"That crowd! Those quitters aren't the Wildcats."

Don turned away. Lots of folks during the previous fortnight had asked him to stay in town. This was the worst of all. "Tom, there's other people mixed in it, too, people who don't really want me to hang on, powerful people, and naturally I don't care to stay when they feel like that."

"You mean Dad and those old dopes?"

Through his anguish Don smiled. He was forced to smile. The boy went on. "Aw, my Dad, he thinks he's Springfield, Indiana. He's got to run everything in this town. You know what, Don? We've been scrapping about the team all winter. But yesterday I told him please in the future to let basketball in this place alone. Was he sore! Trouble is, no one in town stands up to Dad."

"Peedad Wilson does." He wondered how the boy would react to the name.

"There's a guy ain't afraid of Dad." There was almost admiration in his tones. "He's got Dad's number, that little old guy has. He's not scared to buck him; only he's all alone, he has no one to help him. In this town if you don't string along with Dad, you're licked before you start." They were almost Peedad's words, and Don winced as the boy continued. "I told Dad yesterday please to let basketball here alone. Wants to boss every-thing and everyone, even the Wildcats. They're your Wildcats, not his. I asked him why he didn't mind his own business."

The thought of the young Shaw and the elder Shaw, both tough customers, at each other's throats caused Don to smile. He could see— and hear—the battle.

"Tom, boy, it isn't only your father. It's the School Board and almost all the men downtown. They're dead against me."

"The boys sorta hoped maybe you'd think it over and change your mind. Don't the kids count with you, Don? They always usta."

This was no fun. It was more difficult to say no to Tom Shaw than anyone in town, even Pee-dad Wilson. He found himself wondering, and because he wondered he wasn't so sure of himself. "But look! You boys are through; you won't any of you be back in school next winter."

"So what! There's lots of Wildcats coming along, Don—the freshmen, the B team, the subs. They're Wildcats, too, aren't they? We all want them to work with you because you're different; you have the right slant on things. You wouldn't let the Chamber of Commerce buy this boy Kates and bust up our team."

"I'm sorry, Tom. I've agreed to go to Yale."

"I know all that. But the boys hoped you might change your mind, Don. They sent me here, they asked me to give you this." For the second time in his short stay at Springfield the Wildcats presented their coach with a signed letter. Unlike the first, this was an appeal not an ultimatum.

•

We, the undersigned, members of the Springfield varsity, respectfully urge you to reconsider your decision to coach at Yale. We hope you will change your mind and stay in Springfield with the Wildcats.

Tom Shaw, Capt. and No. 5
Jim Turner, No. 9
John Little, No. 11
Walt MacDonald, No. 4
Chuck Foster, No. 12

Don read it, folded it up, and placed it carefully in his purse. The big blue-eyed boy watched every movement. Don looked at him—keen, young, strong.

What makes the J. Frank Shaws in this world, he thought. Once the old man was like Tom; once he looked this way, felt this way, was fresh, young, and keen. Now he is J. Frank Shaw of Springfield, the man who runs the town. If you want anything in Springfield, see J. Frank.

"Tom, boy, see here. If there's one thing could make me change my mind, it's this, believe me. I'd like to stay, 'cause I love the place and I love you kids."

"If you mean that, then why don't you stay?"

"Tom, there's a whole lot you wouldn't understand. Besides, I've sort of promised to go."

The big boy turned his wide blue eyes upon him. For a second Don was back in the Wildcat dressing room before the game, and Jim and

Walt and Chuck and John were there before him on the bench, and Tom was standing up back of them staring with those round eyes, just as he was now.

And Don was looking directly at him. "Tom, you gotta be a smart captain out there to-night . . . you gotta grab that ball . . . you're boss, remember; you take charge . . . you gotta go. Tom, I'm counting on you."

Now Tom was counting on him.

Tom was speaking again, his voice high and strained. "Oh, what's the use? Dad's got this place sewed up; he has this town licked. There's no one can stand up to him. Maybe he's right! Maybe he was right all along. Maybe we should have hired Kates. Maybe we should have done all the things he wanted."

"No, no, Tom. You're wrong, Tom. That's no way to talk, boy; you know better'n that."

"But you're through. We lost the State and you're leaving. You're a quitter."

No one had ever called him that to his face. "Who's a quitter?" He edged closer to the tall boy towering above, tense and angry. Yet not as angry as Don. "Who's a quitter?"

"You! You're leaving, aren't you? And you're

the only one we had, the only person in town. I'm through. I'm not going to scrap any . . ." The boy's voice broke on a sob.

From the distance came sounds. The sounds grew louder. Around the next corner came the strains of the Wildcat song.

"What's that?"

"The kids. The kids and the band. They wanted to take you to the station."

"I'd rather they didn't."

"They wanted to. They're coming now."

The throaty roar of several hundred strong voices came into the room.

"Fight—fight—Wildcats!" Boom! went the drum.

Suddenly Don's own voice sounded in his ears, his voice as he talked to the mob the night of the last game. "And they lost," he heard himself shouting. "They lost. So you've quit!"

Outside, the band and the parade came to a standstill and grouped round the house. They were still singing.

"Fight—fight—Wildcats!" Boom! went the drum.

"As we roll . . . toward the goal . . ."

There was a moment of silence in the room.

Don walked over to the window and looked out, his back to Tom. Suddenly he whirled, came back and stood facing him.

"Look, Tom." Don spoke slowly. "The way I feel at present, I'm plenty sick of basketball. I hardly know's I'll ever want to coach in a town like this again, even did they all want me. But you're right; if I leave now, I'm quitting. So if you think the kids need me round here, I might make some arrangements, I might stay on for . . ."

"Whoopee! You'll stick with us? You'll stay, Don? You mean it?"

"Yep, I could get a job in town, I guess."

"Oh, boy, will those kids out there go wild when they know you're going to stay in Springfield. Yea! Wildcats!" He sprang for the door to tell the crowd outside. Then he turned a second. "Say! With someone like you to help, Don, this town could be different, it could be changed."

Peedad, who had spent all his life fighting Tom Shaw's father, said it better. Though both the young man and the old man meant the same thing.

It could be a city good enough for Lincoln.